Passenger

* * *

Billy Cowie

PASSENGER

*   *   *

BILLY COWIE

Published in Great Britain in 2008 by
Old Street Publishing Ltd,
28–32 Bowling Green Lane, London EC1R 0BJ,
www.oldstreetpublishing.co.uk

A CIP catalogue record for this book is available from the British Library.

ISBN13: 978-1-905847-44-0

Printed and bound in Great Britain by Cromwell Press, Trowbridge, Wiltshire
10 9 8 7 6 5 4 3 2 1

'I am a passenger
And I ride and I ride
I ride through the city's backside
I see the stars come out of the sky
Yeah, they're bright in a hollow sky
You know it looks so good tonight
Singin' la la, la la, la-la-la la
La la, la la, la-la-la la
La la, la la, la-la-la la, la-la'

from *The Passenger* by Iggy Pop

'Paganini was fond of and may even have invented the technique of Fleischton. This is the practice where the violinist uses the fleshy part of the finger to stop the note rather than the callused tip of the finger thereby producing a particularly sweet sound. The technique must be used sparingly as on the one hand it is extremely painful, especially on the very high notes, and secondly if overused then that part of the finger becomes callused and the effect is lost. 'Just as in life and love' the young Paganini would comment.'

from *The Young Paganini* by Edwin Müller

1

MILAN swishes his loosened bow through the air to blow the rosin off. Most of the rest of the orchestra have left after the afternoon rehearsal and only a few stragglers remain.

He glances over to the deserted wind section. Karen has moved down a few chairs to the seat normally occupied by one of the bassoonists – she has her head tilted back into a tiny ray of sunshine.

He looks up. A small window in the high roof is letting through a beam of sun almost like a spotlight, the dust and rosin defining the path all the way down to Karen's face.

He has been waiting for a moment like this for several weeks but there always seemed to be too many people around. She is Japanese, maybe ten years younger than him, thirty-three or four? She wears a lot of eye make-up; it looks a bit kabuki-ish with her shiny black hair and fringe. He puts down his bow and moves over through the chairs. He sits down two seats away from her.

'Hi – I'm Milan.'

'Hi.'

She does not open her eyes or move her head but continues her mini sunbathing.

'You're Karen?'

'I been wondering who I was.'

Funny girl, Milan thinks.

'Do you want to go for coffee or something?'

'Sure.'

She slowly raises her head and pops her eyes open.

'Why not?' she adds with just a flash of a smile that he could have missed had he blinked.

'Just got to get my violin packed up.'

Milan indicates his seat.

She nods and resumes her position, leaning her head back and closing her eyes again.

'Give me whistle when you ready,' she says. 'You know how to whistle don' you?'

'Yes,' he answers, 'You just put your lips together and blow.'

Milan blunders a couple of chairs over on his way back to his seat, like a twelve-year-old kid or maybe Norman Wisdom.

'Mind chairs,' she sings out.

'Thanks,' he replies.

He feels strangely, but not uncomfortably, that she is entirely in control.

They begin a long trek through the barren wastes of Mile End looking for a coffee place. Karen's bit of September sun seems to have melted away and there is something of a chill in the air. The orchestra gets cheap rehearsal space out here and it's no wonder why. Where they were rehearsing before, near Oxford Street, they would have been flooded with Starbucks and Costas, but out here there is nothing.

He puts his foot on the edge of the pavement and his ankle turns over. He nearly falls.

'Easy tiger,' she says grabbing his arm.

Milan limps on but she doesn't let go. Finally they come to a cafe called The Greasy Spoon. He hopes the name is ironic. Unfortunately it's not. It is, in fact, factual. They even have those transparent cups he hates, the ones with a greasy film on them.

Despite this, he is surprisingly hungry all of a sudden. Maybe it's nerves. He has managed to get a cheese roll, which is also on a see-through plate, and a cappuccino of sorts. Karen's got a straight black coffee.

She makes a wry face. At first he thinks it is the coffee but she carries on with, 'Did you hear my mistake in second movement?'

'No,' he lies. (He thinks he is a good liar, good in the sense of proficient. What he does is just sort of relax into the lie, not caring about it, as if it were somehow not connected to him. It seems to work). Of course he heard it.

Karen knows he is being polite.

'Very kind of you, but our dear conductor gave me such a look when I missed that note. You don' know how lucky you are among that crowd of violins. You could be playing *Star Spangled Banner* for all anyone would know.'

She is stirring her coffee with her left hand although she didn't put any milk or sugar in.

'Thanks,' Milan answers, 'it's nice to feel important.'

He actually has tried playing just any old thing in the orchestra before – in a Brahms symphony once, to see if anyone could tell. The conductor managed to notice a slight shading of something not quite right but nothing to put his finger on. Milan's wrong notes were diluted in a sea of right ones. But his playing partner, Daphne, noticed immediately. 'Stop pissing around will you – I want to get home tonight,' she whispered to him without losing a note.

'Do you like flute?' Karen asks him out of the blue. Milan wonders if he has been in dreamland for the last few minutes and more importantly has Karen noticed? Focus, he tells himself.

He answers her, 'What flute? Your flute, or flutes in general, or what?'

'Flute in general.'

He is not really a flute lover but as he is talking to a professional flute player he tones down his response. He also resists the urge to mimic her *frute* pronunciation. He tries to give a balanced response.

'Well, to me, sometimes flutes can sound a touch bland, but in the right hands…'

Karen stops him.

'It OK; I not that keen on flute myself. I prefer saxophone.'

'You play the saxophone?'

'Yes, it same fingering as flute.'

'Not same as clarinet?'

He's starting to lose his *the*-s under her Japanese influence, next he will be involuntarily *r*-ing his *l*-s and *l*-ing his *r*-s.

'No, clarinet overblow octave fifth, flute and sax just octave, clarinet cylinder, sax conical.'

'But flute is cylindrical?'

Despite losing his articles Milan is going to hang onto his verbs at least.

'Yeah, but flute not end stopped.'

He holds his hands up in surrender.

'I give in. Whatever you say.'

She laughs.

'Clever old Adolphe, eh?'

'Adolphe?'

'Adolphe Sax.'

'Oh yes. That Adolphe. Come to think of it, you don't see many Adolphes around these days.'

'Can't think why,' she laughs again.

They hit an awkward pause. He bites his roll.

This silence won't do. With an effort he leaps back into conversation.

'Where are you from?'

'I from Japan.' He doesn't know if she is making fun of him or not.

'I know you're from Japan. I mean where in Japan?'

'Hiroshima,' she says without blinking.

Whoops. Just keep going, he thinks.

'I've heard of that place.'

'Yes, it quite famous.'

'Coming from there. It must be strange?'

'It just big city, like Birmingham or something.' She shrugs her shoulders.

'Maybe not so much strange living there, I mean, but when you're somewhere else telling someone, like just now. You couldn't really say anywhere more startling, could you?'

Karen thinks for a moment.

'Auschwitz?'

He has to nod.

'Yep, that would do it.'

Karen looks at her watch and gets up quickly.

'I late – I late – for very important date,' she sings, getting her things together.

Milan feels a slightly panicky feeling, something in that reedy voice and those *m*-s missing from the *I'm*-s and that hint of the *r* in the *l*-s – it's just like in that book *Catcher in the Rye* when the kid says some women do the tiniest thing and you fall for them.

She does a slight bow.

'Bye-bye Milan san.'

'Shall we do this again?' he says putting in a lot of casual *it doesn't really matter* into his voice, almost an *I wouldn't care if we never met again* thing.

'Sure thing, cowboy.' She takes a last standing sip from her cup.

Milan finishes his roll and coffee and watches her leave with her flute. As she passes the window she does a kind of fish kiss to him with a little smile.

It is eleven o'clock next morning. Andreas has turned up at Milan's place with a bag of croissants. As usual he clambers over piles of papers on the stairs.

'One day someone will die on these stairs and then you'll go to prison.'

Milan changes the subject.

'You look different. New glasses?' Andreas wears expensive designer glasses and is always buying new ones. He is a couple of years younger than Milan and very well turned out.

'Nice, aren't they?'

'You are a fashion victim.'

Andreas thinks for a minute.

'Better a fashion victim than a fashion casualty.'

Milan makes coffee. They sit out on Milan's balcony, of which he is very proud. A flat with a balcony in central London, who ever heard of that, certainly not rented by a penniless musician? It is a bit chilly however.

Andreas puts two sugars in his coffee; he notices Milan's mood.

'You look happy.'

'I met someone.'

'Want to give me the details?' Andreas gets out an imaginary notebook and pencil and studiously licks the point.

'She's female.'

'Female,' Andreas repeats, writing it down carefully.

'She play flute, she called Karen, she Japanese.'

Andreas takes it in and takes it down. Then he thinks a bit.

'That doesn't sound like a very Japanese name, Karen?'

He tries saying it with an *l*, 'Kalen?', but is still not satisfied.

'Her father was a Carpenters fan apparently,' Milan explains.

Andreas hears this information and responds with a couple of lines from *Calling Interplanetary Craft* something or other. Milan emphatically takes no notice and eventually Andreas goes on.

'Does she speaka da English? Or does she talk the *international language of love*?'

Andreas modulates his voice into a passable Barry White impression. He is certainly on form this morning, annoyingly so in fact.

'She has only indulged me with her English so far. I suspect she talks the international language of love and a bit of Japanese I suppose but so far neither of them to me.'

Andreas writes and mouths silently at the same time, 'Nothing to report, so far,' and snaps his imaginary book shut.

'So. What did you two talk about then?'

'Oh, you know, Auschwitz, Hiroshima, Adolphe.'

Andreas nods wisely.

'Always best to play safe with conversation topics on a first date.'

'I don't even know if it was a date, really,' Milan replies rather ruefully.

They sit back in their chairs. Not many more days out here this year Milan is thinking.

'And so where are we up to then?'

'She blew me a kiss.'

'That's promising.'

'And another thing – something about the way she talks, it reminds me of that girl in *Gregory's Girl*.' Milan is thinking of the way she says *cowboy* and *tiger* and maybe just a certain playfulness.

Andreas shakes his head despairingly.

'Well that's got to be fatal; you haven't a chance if she's up to those tricks. Just give in and hope for the best.'

There is one chocolate croissant and one spiral with custard left. Milan cuts them both in half to save argument.

He asks a final question.

'What does *san* mean?'

'San?'

'She called me Milan san when she said goodbye.'

Andreas thinks a moment.

'I think it means Mr or a sign of respect. She must have been being ironic.'

'OK. Out.' Milan pushes open the patio door. 'I didn't ask you round here to be insulted.'

Andreas doesn't move.

'You didn't ask me round here at all, actually.'

'Precisely. Precisely.'

That night's concert is finished and they are filing slowly out of the Festival Hall. Milan pushes past the rest of the violins and catches up with Karen. He hasn't spoken to her since their coffee outing.

'Do you want to go for a drink?'

This is crunch time. She turns softly.

'Oh, sorry, I have hot date with first trombone.'

Milan has been preparing for this response and reacts automatically without even taking in the details.

'Oh. Well never mind.' He starts to move away when he sees something in her expression.

'Only kidding. I glad to come,' she laughs.

She has a nice laugh. She looks good in her black concert dress. There was no flute mistake tonight. She is relieved, happy and confident, and she is going for a drink – with him, what's more.

On the way to the pub Milan recalls that the first trombone is actually a woman. She is small, she is teetotal, she has perfectly formed normal lips – in fact she is the antimatter of trombonists. Milan wonders if this thought is sexist (probably), sizest (more than likely), trombonist (definitely).

They end up in the Yellow Caravel, a nautical pub with netting and seaweed all over the place but more importantly booths and even more importantly, where none of the rest of the orchestra ever go. They have had three drinks, three pints of lager each.

'I thought that Japanese people couldn't drink a lot? Something genetic.'

She empties her pint glass contemptuously and wipes her mouth with her sleeve dramatically.

'Look on and wonder.'

Milan does both.

'I expect you like milk as well then?'

She makes a face.

'No milk. Make me feel sick just thinking about it.'

'OK, no milk then.'

She looks expectantly into her empty glass.

Milan decides now is as good a time as any.

'Can I kiss you?'

He has to ask this question. In films and books and things they never ask permission to kiss; they just seem to look into each other's eyes telepathically and drift together, no problem. Well, if you're honest, they have read the script – they know the next line; they know what's coming. What if you drift in for the first time with the wrong idea and the other person is thinking something completely different and suddenly someone looms into their face – how embarrassing would that be? Better to ask and the other can simply say no thank you and you can swiftly carry on the conversation and never mention it again, ever.

'Sure,' she answers.

They kiss.

Three hours later Milan and Karen are lying in post-coital-bliss (well maybe not bliss, but definitely post-coital-something-good), in her bed at her flat near Earl's Court.

'I heard you were married?' she asks impulsively.

So she has been making inquiries, Milan thinks.

'I still am – technically,' he answers.

He shivers. This is a bit sudden.

'What happened?'

'Alice, her name was Alice. She left me, went away, said bye-bye.' Milan doesn't go into the details.

Next day is a big rehearsal. Milan nearly drops off half way through, rather surprisingly as they are working on the *Rite of Spring* and the percussion section are making something of a meal of all that banging and thumping. Daphne nudges him a cue every so often.

'Too much bed and not enough sleep?' she hints with a wicked look in her eyes.

Milan shrugs, waves of hangover and tiredness alternating in his brain.

'News travels fast in orchestraland, doesn't it?' Not really so surprising as Karen and he did stagger late into the rehearsal together, both looking the worse for wear. 'Actually, I haven't been sleeping properly – and not because of what you think. Or not just because of what you think.'

Daphne has been his orchestral team-mate for three years. Milan asked her out the first time they sat together. *OK if my husband and two kids come?* she answered. Oops. They've since been stuck seated together in the violin section horse race, even moving up three places over as many years, with everyone wanting to get to that front row. Not to the leader's seat mind you, that's specially appointed, but if you get to sit next to him and he gets run over you're there, shaking hands with Rostropovich, getting your own sprinkle of applause and playing solo in *Lark Ascending*.

Daphne sits on the outside, naturally, nearest the audience. The orchestra is concerned about how few women are in it so any it has it likes to put up front, a bit like when you buy an egg sandwich and all the egg is near the edge and inside is just a tiny bit of lettuce. Daphne is the egg and he's the lettuce, Milan supposes.

'Enjoy it while it lasts,' she answers a bit too enviously. Milan thinks maybe he should have persevered with her all those years ago. Anyway, he is invited for dinner back at Karen's place this evening.

She lives in a tiny flat – this visit Milan has more chance to take it in. The main room is spartan in its simplicity.

'Moshi moshi, Karen san,' he says to her. He heard the *moshi moshi* thing in some film.

'Moshi moshi,' she says back laughing.

'Is that wrong?' Milan asks.

'Not exactly, it sweet. Moshi moshi you say when you answer telephone.'

He has brought flowers and wine.

'You don't have much furniture or stuff.'

She starts work on the flowers.

'I only just moved in.'

Milan nods. He thinks, even once she has been here three years there won't be much more.

She pours him a glass of wine and then starts cooking.

'I got good news,' she calls out from her mini kitchen.

'What is it?' Milan shouts through.

'Two days ago, when I had to go, remember, I went for audition to other orchestra.'

Let it be another London orchestra is his immediate thought.

'But you only just started with our one.'

'This early music one. I get to play wooden flute.'

'I presume they took you?'

'Yeh, I jus' heard.'

Milan squeezes into the small space behind her.

'I suppose it's congratulations then. When do you start?'

'I have four week notice with your lot. Maybe I could get you job with this new one?'

Milan shakes his head.

'No, not for me, thanks; I like my vibrato too much for that authentic mob.'

Milan is relieved to discover this early music bunch are based in London but is nevertheless a bit disappointed. He had been imagining a future of no more lonely hotel rooms on tour.

They have soup and then sushi she has made herself.

'No meat, no brains, no fishy, jus' as ordered.'

'Delicious,' Milan responds.

'I don' eat much meat anyway; I like fish though.'

'Whale?' he asks cheekily.

'Whale not fish, you silly boy,' he is corrected.

She continues.

'Whale taste very nice but I don' eat it. Save planet, you know.' They drink to the planet.

After dinner Milan discovers her CD collection behind a sliding panel. They play *name that tune in one*. He plays the first note of a track and she guesses what the piece is. She is surprisingly accurate. It is amazing how much you can pick up from just the first sound; you would think there could be only so many first notes in the world. She gets *Virginia Plane* from Roxy Music straight away, as with *Tristan and Isolde*. Then she hesitates with *Like a Virgin*. She knows it is Madonna but thinks it is maybe *Holiday*. *Nessun Dorma* immediately. They are her CDs of course; maybe it would be more of a test to try her on his. He notices there are no Carpenters CDs, which reminds him of something.

'You know that stuff about your name and the Carpenters and your parents?'

Milan sits back down with her on her futon.

'Yeh,' she answers warily.

'So, how old are you?'

'That rather personal question. I thirty-two.'

'You don't look it,' Milan says automatically, although she does in fact look younger anyway.

'Thank you.'

'That means that you were born in sixty-six, but the Carpenters didn't get famous 'til the seventies.' Milan tilts his head questioningly.

'Karen not my real name. I got fed up spelling my real name all time and nobody say it properly anyway. I made it up about Carpenters. My parents Beatles fans actually.'

'So what is your real name then?'

She tells him. Milan asks her to write it down. He doesn't even attempt to say it.

'Karen suits you.' He puts his arm around her.

They kiss for a while.

'Do you want tea?' she asks him eventually.

'No thanks,' he answers. 'A cup of tea is not really my cup of tea.'

'What is your cup of tea then?'

'A cup of coffee is more my cup of tea.'

'We not have coffee. But anyway, this not black tea; this green tea.'

Milan agrees to taste the green tea. He surprises himself by liking it. Actually he quite likes ordinary tea if he's honest. He doesn't know why he said all that other stuff. Sometimes he just says things without knowing why, he really does.

2

MILAN wakes up. It is around half six. Streams of light are filtering through the blinds. They are at Karen's place. He lies there; Karen is sleeping. He can hear her soft breathing. They have been going out for five weeks now and there has not been a harsh word between them – well, a few discussions on his flat and its lack of space and untidiness, and general hygiene standards. She has moved to her new orchestra and seems happy with it. Milan has been to see them a few times and they are good but a bit too wholesome for his taste, a bit like semi-skimmed, whereas he prefers his orchestras full cream.

He enjoys the quietness of the morning for a while and is thinking about slipping back to sleep. And then. Tap tap tap – tap. He hears a clicking sound. It goes on and on. It is the rhythm of Beethoven's fifth symphony, bar after bar, with the counterpoints and accompaniments filled in. He listens for a few minutes and then he gives Karen a push.

'OK, that's a funny game.'

She appears to be struggling out of sleep.

'What is it?'

'Don't pretend, Miss Tapping-fingers.' He shakes his head at her cheek in trying to maintain her innocence.

She turns towards him.

'What?'

'Da da da dah,' Milan sings.

'What time is it?'

She seems to be getting slightly annoyed.

She pulls a hair out of her mouth.

'Were you just tapping there, some Beethoven?' he asks.

'What?'

She then says something in Japanese. Milan doesn't know the word but if he had to guess from the tone of her voice he would go for *asshole*. She turns over and is quickly sleeping again.

He looks at the ceiling where the parallel lines from the window are moving gently. If she had been messing around tapping and so on she wouldn't have got so annoyed. But if it wasn't her? Sounds coming from the neighbours? A dream he had maybe? He starts thinking about how long it's been since they last played the Beethoven. Not for a few years. It used to be programmed all the time. Now it's gone a bit out of fashion. It's turned into a bit of a cliché. Actually Milan sometimes nearly laughs when they do play it. Beethoven cannot be serious. He thinks it would be nice to hear it completely fresh again for the first time, without all the baggage. Maybe some things should be locked away from you when you're little and you only get them when you are really ready for them, like an inheritance. His back is hurting him a bit.

At breakfast Milan apologises to Karen.

'Sorry for waking you about the tapping.'

She is busy with a piece of toast.

'What tapping? You crazy sometimes, you know that?'

Obviously she didn't surface enough earlier on to take his babbling in or even remember it happened. Good, he thinks. Forget about it yourself, Milan.

Two days later he is on a bus going to Vauxhall when he hears more tapping. More Beethoven. This time it takes him a while to recognise the piece just from the rhythm. It is Beethoven symphony number six – second movement. It carries on with its swaying triplety rhythm, not just for a few bars but for the whole of the first section. He sits transfixed way past his stop.

Back home he phones Andreas.

'I think I'm maybe going mad.'

'I could have told you that years ago,' Andreas predictably replies.

'No, seriously.'

Milan explains the two incidents. Andreas listens patiently.

'Just a daydream,' is his verdict.

'Get yourself a proper job. All that scraping, up and down, backwards and forwards, can't be good for you,' Andreas adds helpfully.

The third encounter comes when Milan is in a rehearsal. They are playing a Mozart piano concerto and the tapping is in sync with the pianist. Not tracking along but sometimes anticipating what she is going to play next. Milan actually stops playing long enough to be noticed by their guest Russian conductor.

'Mozart not to your liking?' The Russian is obviously not enjoying himself today. Milan pretends that a string has slipped its tuning.

Eventually Milan phones the clinic on Karen's orders. Three more tapping incidents and he has, not exactly a pain, but a bit of discomfort at the bottom of his back. The orchestra pays for everyone in it to have private medical insurance. Milan always feels guilty about it but at least he gets an appointment in two hours.

The clinic is new and very smart. They even have a coffee machine in the waiting room. A few expensive looking ladies are waiting. They give him a look when he sits down.

Five minutes later the receptionist calls out to him.

'Mr Kotzia, can you take this in with you when you go in? I forgot to put it in earlier with the others.'

She hands him a small cardboard folder stuffed with all his past medical notes. He holds it gingerly on his lap, tempted to have a look through it but feeling strangely guilty about doing so. The folder is also so stuffed he has a vague feeling that if he pulls anything out it will simply explode all over the place. So instead he just examines the front. There is his name, date of birth, place of birth, doctor's name, health number, address, and right at the bottom two blank spaces marked date and place of death. A chill comes over him. One day these blanks will be filled in with some town or other and a time and date, and the wodge of papers will be kept for a while and then disposed of. The receptionist calls his name.

Milan goes in to see Dr Snell. *Schnell* means quick in German he muses but Dr Snell is not quick he knows. When he is examining you he will sometimes pause mid-movement and you think he is trying to find a way to break something to you, *you haf only six months left, I am afraid eet ees incurable* etc. but when he gets round to speaking it is usually *put your shirt back on* and not with a German accent either, more of a Midlands tone. Milan wonders if perhaps Snell is a Buddhist living in the 'now', experiencing intensely the moment of removing his cold stethoscope from Milan's back. Or maybe he is just losing his marbles in a graceful sort of way.

Milan sits down.

Dr Snell is wearing his bow tie again. What kind of

person in this day and age wears a bow tie to work, Milan asks himself? Milan knows that he himself wears a bow tie at concerts, but that is a different matter; it's black for one thing and he has to wear it. Dr Snell has actually chosen to wear his. He got up this morning, looked in his wardrobe and decided *'I think I'll wear the yellow bow tie this morning.'*

'What seems to be the problem, Mr Kotzia?' the doctor asks, without even looking up from his notepad.

That *seems* bothers Milan slightly. Snell always says it, and it sometimes makes Milan wonder if the doctor is hinting that he must be imagining the problem before he has even told him what it is?

Milan answers rather tetchily,

'It *seems* to be a kind of clicking in my back. Down at the base of my spine. This may sound strange but it is a musical clicking, Beethoven usually, Mozart once.'

Dr Snell does this weird thing with his mouth and writes something.

Having to see a doctor when he is not actually ill makes Milan feel a touch aggressive.

'What have you just written there?'

Milan has the hypochondriac's paranoia that his bulging notes are full of *here we go again*-s and *all in his head*-s and strange doctors' codes for *barmy as they come.*

'Just what you said, nothing more, nothing less. Here, take a look.'

- 23 -

Snell wearily turns the notes to him. Sure enough he has written just what he said and no exclamation marks or anything.

'You have nice handwriting, very clear,' Milan remarks.

Snell takes back the notes and sighs.

'Thank you. Let's take a look at your back.'

The doctor gestures to him to pull his shirt up and lie face down on the couch.

'Does this hurt?'

'No.'

A few presses here and there and all of a sudden Snell seems to have lost interest and is busy washing his hands. Milan sits up and puts his clothing back in order.

'I want you to see a colleague of mine, Mr Alex Lister. Lister is good with backs. Mr Lister. Let me just see.'

Snell talks to someone on the phone and then cups his hand over the mouthpiece.

'Tomorrow at two in the X-ray room here and then in to see Mr Lister at three.'

Milan nods. So I'm getting a Mister, he thinks – must be important otherwise I would just be getting a Doctor who is in the second league medically compared to a Mister.

The next day at exactly three Milan enters Mr Lister's office; the X-ray had only taken a few minutes. Then he had sat around drinking coffee for an hour. Milan had wanted to go to the toilet just before his name was called but he is in the door now.

Mr Lister looks about twelve years old with a rather round face and no bow tie, in fact no tie at all. He pushes an X-ray into a light box and speaks while looking at it.

'I read Dr Snell's notes.'

'Yes?'

'We're going to need more X-rays. There is something wrong with this one.'

Milan half stands. Is it OK to look he wonders?

Lister sees him move and gestures him over to the light box. He points at the middle of the picture.

'There's your spine, your ribcage, all OK, but down here,' he points to a jumble of marks, 'the plate is fogged or maybe it's a sort of double exposure. Didn't they do a lateral view?'

Milan tries to make sense of the lines and blobs.

'Lateral?'

'You know – sideways – from the side.'

Lister turns his head sideways. Even in his slight state of shock at seeing his insides exposed Milan gets the hint that Lister thinks he might not understand *sideways* and might even seem to need a vital head clue to grasp the concept.

'Yes, sideways, they did do a sideways one as well.'

Lister phones somebody.

Now he is doing something with his mouth, a different something to Snell. Maybe all doctors do something with their mouths, Milan wonders.

'They kept the lateral plate back, something wrong with that one too. They're bringing it up; it will be here in a minute.'

They both sit down. Lister reads more of Snell's notes.

One of the radiologists Milan had seen before enters with another X-ray, which he puts up against the first. There is a short debate between the two as they go from one picture to the other.

Eventually Lister speaks to Milan.

'John here...'

John helpfully puts his hand up, although there are only the three of them in the room.

'John here has just been pointing out to me that the positioning of the unusual markings on the first slide are consistent with the rotation of your body on the second.'

'Which means?'

'Which means that if there was a fault with the machine or the plates the two pictures wouldn't be consistent. Whatever these marks are, it's inside you and not a fault of the X-ray machine or the operator.'

John is nodding.

'You've never seen anything like it?' Lister asks him.

'Not in twenty years.'

John is going towards the door. Lister stops him, 'I think we need an MRI scan. We haven't got a scanner here. Maybe you can pull a few favours at the Hammersmith?'

John nods confidently and leaves.

Lister turns back to Milan.

'In the meantime let's have a look.'

Milan repeats the shirt up, lying down routine. He has a feeling this is going to happen quite a lot over the next few days.

Lister is more thorough than Snell was.

'In your notes it mentions Beethoven?'

'Yes. Beethoven's fifth symphony, you know it?'

Lister nods. He presses his fingers quite painfully into Milan's back.

'You're a musician?'

'Violinist.'

Now Mr Lister is washing his hands.

'I can't see anything physically wrong at the minute. As for the Beethoven thing, you know we all like to put random patterns into a kind of order, a dripping tap takes on a rhythm or you imagine you see a face on the moon.'

Milan feels slightly patronised by all this *random* and *imagine* and is tempted to say twenty-five bars of music is a big pattern but bites his tongue.

The phone rings – his MRI scan is confirmed for tomorrow at four.

Back at his flat Karen is chopping vegetables. The sink area seems remarkably clean. She has brought her own knives. They look alarmingly sharp and large and she is chopping extremely fast. Milan puts his arms around her from behind.

'Don't you need all your fingers to play the flute?'

She makes a fake accidental chop and holds up her hand with a bent middle finger.

'Oooh ooh ooh!'

Milan looks carefully among the chopped carrots.

'Better find the missing bit; you know I'm a vegetarian.'

She turns round and puts her arms around him.

'Well, Vegetarian san, you going to live?'

'I might just pull through.'

'And?' She places the tip of her big knife on his throat.

'And I have more tests tomorrow, an MRI scan at the Hammersmith Hospital.'

'What about Ludwig – heard any more from him?'

He shakes his head.

She starts chopping again.

'Hey – maybe you been possessed by his spirit like that old lady that was in news.'

Milan stands behind her as she carries on and puts his arms back around her. He really likes the way she says *hey*. Nobody says *hey* these days, do they?

Milan gets to the rehearsal early for once, as he has to leave before the end to get to his hospital appointment. He had also had something of a discussion with Karen the evening before. He had asked her to stay but she finds his place a bit too cluttered. Well, compared to her Zen flat it must seem busy to say the least.

Daphne is reading a novel. He looks at the cover as she carries on reading.

'Isn't that the book about a violinist? I heard it's terrible.'

Daphne turns a page and carries on reading.

'I know, I know, but you've got to read it anyway, haven't you? The guy who wrote it probably spent a week nosing around some orchestra to get his atmosphere. It reminds me of that joke, *what do you call someone who hangs around with musicians?*'

Milan strokes his chin and pretends to think for a few seconds.

'A conductor?'

They both still laugh at that old joke. Rock musicians always say the answer is a drummer but he thinks conductor is funnier.

'Speaking of reading did you ever hear that the Northern Light Orchestra all used to have newspapers on their music stands and would read them as they played in recording sessions,' he continues.

'True professionals,' nods Daphne impressed.

Milan eventually finds the Hammersmith Hospital. Once again he doesn't have to wait. He goes straight in. Gets undressed, puts the green gown on and is then interrogated by a male nurse.

'Do you have a pacemaker?'

'No.'

'Any metal implants of any kind, hip, cranial plate?'

He is tempted to answer *I have this metal bolt through my neck* but instead he gives an apathetic, 'Is this absolutely necessary?'

The nurse gets a bit short with him.

'Just answer the questions. Do you have any idea how strong the magnets are in there or how hot a piece of metal might get?'

At last he is sucked into the white tube. He feels vaguely claustrophobic in the cramped space. He sees some felt pen graffiti on the inside saying *get me out of here* and a little drawing of that scream face. Lister talks to him reassuringly while he is in the machine.

After Milan gets dressed he is taken to a small room. Lister is in there with one of the technicians, who looks a bit Chinese, and John from yesterday, all three sitting in front of a large computer monitor. They sit Milan down next to them; it is a bit of a squash. There are two other technicians standing in the gloom by the door.

'It's best if you see this for yourself,' Lister tells him.

A few clicks and the original X-rays come on the screen transferred somehow into the computer.

'These are the pictures from yesterday, the X-rays. This is your abdomen. Here is what confused us before.'

With a pen connected by an umbilical chord to the computer Lister highlights an area on the screen.

'That is your hipbone, but this dark smudge above it and these lines? We've never seen anything like this before.'

The Chinese guy butts in then.

'The closest I seen is old X-rays of pregnant women – obviously we don' X-ray pregnant women anymore – but the angles are all wrong, plus you' a man.'

'You are a man?' John takes this one up and nearly everyone seems slightly amused.

Milan nods.

'Want me to prove it?'

'No no, we believe you.'

Lister is somewhat annoyed at John's interruption. Milan thinks maybe Lister is compensating for his boyish looks by being cross a lot of the time.

'Anyway, here's the MRI we have just done. I took the liberty of sending it to a colleague of mine in Pennsylvania. He's flying here tomorrow.'

'Just because of me?'

'Yes. I'd do the same if I was him.'

The screen has lit up with a multicoloured image that looks vaguely three-dimensional. Lister seems able to turn and twist the image by moving his pen over a pad. Milan is unable to make sense of the rotating shapes.

Two more technician types poke their heads round the door. It's getting crowded and quite hot in the room.

Lister points with the pen.

'OK, this is your liver. This is one kidney. The other kidney should be here but is pushed up there. Your colon and small intestines are all massively displaced. Have you ever had digestive problems?'

Milan shakes his head.

'That's surprising. And you better not get appendicitis. It would take them a week to find it.'

This time he laughs at his own joke.

'Anyway, this is what's displacing them. Our initial impressions were a very large tumour or cyst of some sort. But it is far too structured. Here, let me superimpose the X-ray.'

The previous black lines magically fit into the bluish mass.

'Ignore the colour, that's artificial, we put that in. Look here. As Hu just said it resembles to a certain extent a foetus, except what might be the skull is significantly enlarged. We see a torso with one fairly developed limb, and one vestigial one. There is nothing resembling legs that I can see and over...'

Milan stops him by holding up his hand in front of the screen.

'Hang on a minute. I don't understand. What are you saying? What is this?'

Lister lets out a long breath before continuing.

'I'm guessing here, but what may have happened is that when you were in the womb there was another fertilised egg. Your developing embryo managed to wrap itself around the other and subsume it.'

'It has happened before, lots of times,' Hu breaks in.

'There was a case in Italy a few years back; a young man had an operation to remove a tumour and they discovered it was a foetus.'

'There also were cases in Russia and India quite recently.'

'A boy of nine in Portland died when the internal foetus grew too large for him to sustain it.'

Everybody and their wives seem to be chipping in.

Milan points at the screen.

'Is this thing alive then?'

Lister waves a dismissive hand.

'No, no, that's not what we're saying. This all happened...'

He glances at Milan's notes.

'...forty-two years ago. It is surprising in a way that it's not more apparent. You aren't particularly fat after all.'

'Thanks,' Milan says.

'It is not actually all that large and is fitted around your spine and organs in a quite beautiful fashion.'

There is a general pause. Milan breaks the silence.

'What now?'

He cannot take his eyes off the small bluish figure.

'We need to do more tests. We would like you back here on Friday. My American colleague will be here by then. We need to find out firstly if this object is threatening you in any way – whether to operate to remove it or leave it where it is.'

Milan meets Andreas in the Windmill pub. Andreas was wearing a kind of cloak thing when he arrived which caused a few turned heads. He has thankfully taken it off. Milan gets them two beers and explains the findings.

'My parents had always wanted a girl, but they got me instead.'

'Shame,' says Andreas unsympathetically.

Milan carries on.

'They were going to call her Roma. Maybe this is her.'

'Roma, that's a nice name. Is that why they called you Milan when you disappointed them by being born a boy?'

'Seems so. In fact it could have been worse. They flirted with the name Romeo for me for a while.'

'Romeo, Romeo, wherefore art thou Romeo?' Andreas declaims rather loudly. Milan feels the heads that turned when he entered swing round again.

'Calm down,' he tells Andreas.

'Romeo. That was a close call. You wouldn't have lasted five minutes at school with a name like Romeo.'

Silence ensues as Milan relives his school days with this new name.

Andreas finally breaks it.

'You really think it's alive, don't you?'

'Well, there has been all that tapping.'

'What's she saying – *let me out, let me out*?'

Milan gives Andreas a look.

'Sorry, sorry. Anyway have you heard any more from her, a bit of Bartok, some jazz?'

Andreas raps playfully if a little warily on the table.

Milan ignores him, distracted by the coincidence of two *let me out*s in one day. He remembers his claustrophobic feelings in the white tube, which wasn't even closed, and he was in there for only thirty minutes. Forty-two years, it doesn't bear thinking about.

On Friday Milan arrives back at the Hammersmith. No delay at all again. He feels vaguely guilty thinking about people with life threatening diseases waiting for months to even get in the door, but he supposes this is new stuff for these doctors. This is conference stuff, articles, even a book. Maybe they could call it *The Man Who Mistook his Sister for his Stomach*.

Lister's American colleague Conrad has turned up, suffering from jet lag but obviously excited Milan is there. Milan gets a hint of something more than just colleagues between them but they keep a professional veneer going. They wire him up so he is unable to move.

Lister explains.

'These things on your back are simple microphones attached to recorders. We want to try and get a bit of clicking down. These on your stomach are neural sensors.

We want to know if there is any neural activity going on down there. Later on we want to do more X-rays after injecting you with special dyes to check how your blood is flowing.'

'None of this will harm her will it?' Milan asks from his weird position. He is tied down like Gulliver.

Lister opens his eyes wide.

'Her?'

Milan explains to Lister his conviction that it may be his long-lost sister Roma inside him. Lister has definitely been considering the possibility that there might be something living inside Milan, otherwise why all this recording and neural stuff, although all he allows himself is a quiet, 'We shall see what we shall see, or should I say, hear what we shall hear.'

Milan lies prone for two and a half hours; no clicks come.

Lister and Conrad are clearly disappointed. They seem to have found faint traces of neural activity but nothing conclusive. The blood tests appear to show that Roma, as Milan now insists she be called, is receiving a substantial blood flow from his system, but once again nothing really conclusive.

They all have a short conference at five after a long day.

Lister takes the lead. Conrad watches him intently; definitely something going on there Milan thinks.

'Well the first thing to say is that having re-examined all the previous tests and taking into account the long-term nature of this situation – you know it's been there more than forty years – we don't feel that you are in any particular danger at present. The cyst...'

Lister sees Milan's expression.

'I mean Roma, as you would like to name her, is quite a substantial object and surgical removal is not a straightforward process. Also given your conviction that this Roma may be conscious complicates the issue. If she is in any sense of the word alive I am fairly certain that removal from your body would kill her. For a start her blood system is intimately connected with yours and secondly, to be frank, there is such a lot missing that it would be impossible to sustain her even with the most intensive life support.'

More tests are scheduled for the following week.

Milan leaves the hospital feeling woozy from the injections and sits down on a wall nearby. He hears tapping.

'Well, that's a bit late isn't it?' he says, though he is not exactly sure who he is talking to.

It's the *William Tell Overture*, the end section. Milan decides to join in, tapping lightly on his hipbone. Roma leaves a few gaps, he fills them in and they race towards an exciting climax.

Either she is in there, Milan decides, or else I am in some kind of serious mental trouble.

3

O N Sunday Karen arrives at Milan's place at ten in the morning unannounced. She has her hair scraped back and is wearing a black poloneck jersey and no make-up. Milan is at first pleasantly surprised to see her, thinking she just found him so irresistible that she couldn't wait 'til this evening, when they had arranged to meet.

He soon sees from her expression though that she is bearing bad news.

'Read that.'

She gives him one of the Sunday papers folded over on an inside story.

The headline reads, *Man claims living twin inside.*

Milan scans the story and is relieved that there is no name given.

A forty-two-year-old man was discovered at a west London clinic last week to have the remains of his twin inside him. The technical term for this is 'foetus in fetu', a rare form of conjoined twins. The man claims that the twin is alive and sends him messages by clicking the rhythms of pieces of music but doctors remain sceptical about the possibility that the twin could still be alive after forty-two years.

Milan reads the whole story again.

'Shit. At least there is not much detail and they haven't got my name.'

Milan allows Karen to enter the flat at last. She clambers over the piles of rubbish but wisely, in view of the circumstances, refrains from saying anything about them.

She takes the paper and reads the story again herself.

'It probably only matter of time 'til they find out who you are.'

Milan sits down. He feels tired. He slept only a few hours last night. The only people he has told about what's going on are Andreas and Karen. Neither would have said anything to anyone without asking him.

'The story must have come from someone at the hospital,' he concludes.

Milan sends Karen out for the rest of the Sunday papers and they plough through them but none of the others has picked up the piece.

On Monday first thing Milan phones Lister. Milan is furious about the leaking of the news, which is in every paper this morning. All the articles are more or less a copy of the day before's thing, some with a few extra dismissive comments from medical people added in. There are very few details but the story seems to be slightly longer each time he finds it.

Mr Lister has seen the articles and is very calm and apologetic. He is trying to find out who gave out the story. He thinks one of the technicians in another department may have overheard something. He cautions Milan that something like this is so startling that it is almost inevitable that it will quickly become news. Angrily Milan cancels the remaining tests. Lister doesn't sound surprised but asks him to reconsider his decision at any time.

That evening at around ten the telephone rings. Milan has just got a new number and only six people have it but he is still a bit wary about picking up the phone. He decides to answer. It's Andreas.

'Put the TV on – Channel 4 – now. Call you back later.'

Andreas hangs up.

Milan dutifully switches on. It's a late night chat show. The hostess is half-way through introducing an American. A *fraud-buster* she calls him and the band she has plays the *Ghostbusters* film music as he enters down some stairs. She is sitting behind her desk in a very smart dark suit, and the fraud-buster, Al Cooper seems to be his name, wearing a bow tie a lot flashier than Dr Snell's and a satisfied expression, sits down on a sofa next to her desk.

'So, Al,' she starts out, 'what've you got for us this week?' He seems to be a regular feature.

'OK, Simone, how about a forty-year-long pregnancy and with the bearer a man?'

Simone? The name seems vaguely familiar. Milan hasn't been watching much television recently. She feigns amazement.

'We've all been reading about this guy with another living person inside him.'

Al nods in a knowing kind of way.

'A so-called living person. This is a really clever one, Simone.'

Simone turns to the camera straight on.

'Well, we're clever too. We've managed to track him down. Mr Milan Kotzia is his name.'

She rolls the words of his name around her mouth. Milan feels something rather shocking at hearing his name on television, something about the weight of millions of viewers watching.

Simone turns back to the American.

'But tell me Al, isn't there serious scientific evidence for his claim?'

'According to my sources there is evidence that this guy has something inside him, could be a tumour, cyst or whatever. No big news there. The real question is whether this thing's alive.'

Simone scans her research notes.

'But he seems to have felt a particular clicking? Is there a kind of communication there?'

'Exactly. Well I've brought a young friend along, Lana, thirteen, from the Romanian State Circus. She knows something about clicking.'

Simone turns back to camera. That direct look into camera again, it makes Milan realise why he hates these kinds of show.

'Lana from Romania, let's bring her in.'

Simone starts clapping, signalling a burst of audience applause.

Lana enters. She looks even less than the claimed thirteen but smiles confidently. The audience applauds even more. She is wearing a sequinned circus outfit and is just this side of anorexic.

Simone has come out from behind her desk.

'Lana, what do you do?'

Lana looks back at Simone blankly. Al jumps in to save the day.

'Why don't we let her show us? Actions speak louder than words.'

The American gestures her to the front of the audience. The girl takes up a position near a row of microphones in her bright spangly outfit. She closes her eyes. She makes a slight head movement and a crack, surprisingly, rings out. The entire audience winces. She sets up a rhythmic pulsing of smaller clicks coming from her right shoulder, and then counterpoints them with more of the neck noises. A few bars later she adds in other sounds – from her feet? The display lasts only a few minutes. The audience goes wild. Lana smiles shyly.

Simone is impressed. Applauding, she rounds up the section.

'So, Mr Milan Kotzia, if you are watching perhaps you would like to come in and match that.' The programme dissolves into adverts.

Milan turns off the set.

He rings Karen. She has been forewarned by Andreas too and has also seen the programme.

'Can I stay at your place for a couple of days?' he asks.

Milan grabs some clothes. When he gets to the end of the street he looks back towards his door. Two reporters and a photographer are ringing his bell. Milan is stunned at the speed of all this. It's hardly two weeks since he first noticed the clicking and now this. How did they get his name so fast and that Romanian girl and everything?

Round at Karen's place they discuss strategies.

Karen is for bluffing it out.

'If you hide away they think that there something going on.'

She makes him green tea.

'So you think I should just act as normal?'

'It blow over. As far as everyone knows you have strange tumour. Big deal. My uncle had big tumour, size of watermelon. He keep it in jar now. But everything else?

No one has heard clicking except you? Maybe it just your imagination.'

Milan detects a slight hint in her voice that even Karen might think it is just his imagination.

He can see no alternative to her plan of toughing it out, though. The more he hides away the more fuel it will add to the speculation.

On Tuesday evening Milan goes back to his flat.

Outside the door there are around a dozen journalists.

One reads his name carefully from a note pad.

'Are you Milan Kotzia?'

'That's me.'

Milan stops and smiles.

Inside he's not smiling. But Milan is under the strictest of instructions. The keener you are, the more publicity seeking, the less people will be interested, his advisors, that's Andreas and Karen, have told him. Well, that's their theory anyway.

Another journalist butts in.

'What's this about having a living person inside you?'

'You believe everything you read in the papers?' Milan is rather pleased with himself for this off-the-cuff response. The irony is not lost on the journalists – a couple of them even smile.

He carries on, on a roll.

'I had back pains. Had a few X-rays; they found a

tumour, quite large, not life threatening, unusual shape.'

Milan has his key in the lock. Don't hurry he reminds himself.

'We heard something about clicking?'

'Yeah,' another joins in, 'clicking and music?'

Milan puts his hand to his ear. Don't get too theatrical, he thinks to himself.

'You hear any clicking?'

The journalist shrugs. His friend takes over.

'Can we take a couple of pictures?'

Milan brushes his coat down a bit.

'Sure, go ahead, is my hair OK?'

Milan pats his hair down. He is still smiling on the outside.

'Are there no television people here yet?'

The photographer takes a few extra pictures.

'They're always two steps behind us. Probably turn up tomorrow.'

On the way to the Wednesday rehearsal Milan picks up a couple of papers. A few have his picture in them but not on the front page, and not very big. He can already see the story starting to run out of steam. There is actually more mention of the Romanian girl on Monday's television show; some doctors think she could be damaging her bones. There is even talk of child cruelty and immigration issues.

At the hall the chairman of the orchestra committee, George, takes him aside.

'What's going on Milan?' he asks him kindly.

They have been friends for three years. George is *number one percussion player* as Karen says so beautifully. He is quite large and always looks as if his suit is one size too small for him.

'This publicity is all a storm in a teacup, George.'

George shakes his head.

'I don't mean the publicity, Milan. You know us. We'll take anything we can get in that department. Maybe you could mention our next concert when you talk to them again.'

They sit down. George carries on.

'No. I mean what about you; are you all right? Is this, whatever it is, dangerous? Do you need time off or anything?'

'*Alles in ordnung.* I'm not even going for more tests anymore. In fact I'm as fit as a fiddle.'

George laughs politely at Milan's joke and then takes his arm in a surprisingly intimate gesture.

'Just let me know, OK?'

During the rehearsal Milan notices a few disguised glances from the brass section but there are no comments apart from Daphne's, 'How are we today?' when she sits down next to him.

'We are well,' Milan answers regally.

Back at Milan's flat the phone rings. Surprisingly the journalists don't seem to have got his number. Milan picks it up, under instruction to act normal under all circumstances.

'Hello, Kotzia, the human overcoat speaking.'

'Hello Mr Kotzia, this is Alex Conway, Professor Alex Conway. Mr Lister gave me your number.'

Despite her name the caller is definitely a woman.

Milan nearly puts the phone down immediately.

'I told Lister that I didn't want any more tests.'

'I don't do tests. I'm a behavioural psychologist. I'm interested in your case. I might be able to give you advice on communication.'

She has a very crackly voice. Milan tries to work out her age, about fifty he guesses.

'What do you mean?'

An eloquent pause on the phone.

'Maybe your Roma has something to say.'

Milan feels an instant negative reaction against this manipulative use of Roma's name but at the same time it undeniably draws him in.

'You believe that she is alive?'

'Well, you seem to think so. Lister didn't think you were delusional.'

Delusional? Milan thinks to himself. Just what kind of conversations have all these doctors been having about him?

Milan reluctantly makes an appointment to see her. He is still angry with Lister and company but is suddenly filled with a strange kind of excitement. This professor's comments have opened up a whole world of possibilities Milan hadn't even considered. All this business with the reporters and newspapers seems to have faded into the background. He realises that up to now he hasn't given a moment's thought to his sister.

4

Oɴ Wednesday morning just after ten Milan finds Professor Conway's office. It is in a university building in north London, on the fourteenth floor. She is standing by the window looking out at quite an impressive view. Milan can make out the Post Office Tower and maybe Big Ben somewhere in the distance.

'Professor Conway?' Milan asks.

'Come in,' she answers.

'Any relation?'

'To whom?'

'You know, Russ Conway, the piano player with a finger missing, played *Side Saddle*.'

She is nodding.

'I know who you mean. He is a cousin of mine, rather distant. I met him once.'

They sit down.

'I don't know how much you know about all this, my sister, I mean?'

'I probably know more about our little friend than you do.'

She gestures towards a blue clip-file on her desk. Milan wonders briefly whether patient confidentiality has gone out of the window these days.

He decides to ignore this thought and jump in at the deep end with a question.

'You said something about communication on the phone?'

'Well, if you are right about the tapping, Mr Kotzia, it's already started. What we need to do is make it a two-way thing.'

'How do you suggest we do that?'

Conway stretches her hands in front of herself. She talks very quickly.

'The first thing we need to determine is exactly what Roma's world is like, what she experiences, if we are to communicate with her, that is.'

It is obvious that the professor has already given this much thought before Milan came but the words flood out as if she is making it up as she goes along.

'You're the expert,' is all he can think to say. This talk of *worlds* and *experiences* seems surreal to him.

'Let's start with what we know. The first thing is her hearing. Obviously she must have a form of auditory ability. We know this from the tapping of rhythms, the Beethoven that you heard. It could be that she is unable to hear different pitches and is only responding to rhythm. I think this is unlikely however. She is obviously hearing through your body tissue so this would drastically change the sound characteristics but she is probably compensating for that. Also she probably hears a lot of you...'

Milan interrupts her.

'Wait, wait, slow up now.'

Conway is speaking faster and faster and what she is saying seems very dense and weird. Milan is again conscious of how little thought he has given to the whole area of his sister's experience. He has been completely wrapped up in his own world, ironically.

'Can you explain what you mean by *a lot of me*?'

Conway temporarily slows down a bit.

'Have you ever put your ear up against someone's stomach?'

Milan shakes his head, but the professor hardly notices and continues.

'We are noisy creatures, what with digestion, blood flow – even neural activity produces some sound.'

Milan feels he should have brought a notebook.

'OK, so we have hearing. What else is there?'

'Well, I'm guessing a bit here – we can be almost certain she has no sight at all, also no smell, no taste, no touch – apart from her touching your spine. In addition she may be motion aware, for example when you walk, when you move up or down, your spatial position, that would all depend on her inner-ear development, which itself may be tied to vision and touch, in which case it might not be developed. She may have sensitivity to temperature but massively shielded by your body. I would imagine she would know if you got in a hot bath for example. Then of course there is your blood chemistry. She must be sharing your blood so whatever you get in terms of blood chemistry she gets too.'

'Such as?'

'I would say probably the greatest impact is your blood sugar level. For example you eat a piece of chocolate and your blood sugar goes up; you feel good, so does she. Then your insulin levels go up and soak up all the blood sugar; you feel low, so does she. I suppose it's important to stress that the blood chemicals just come out of the blue for her. She is not aware of chocolate taste or anything, just a flood of abstract chemicals. Then as well as sugar there is caffeine, nicotine – all the usual suspects and not forgetting our old friend alcohol.'

She leaves a slight gap and Milan leaps in.

'You think she gets drunk?'

'In terms of blood chemistry, whatever you get then she gets too. Maybe you could see if her rhythmic tapping gets more erratic after you've had a few?'

'And hangovers?'

The professor smiles.

'No gain without the pain.'

Milan is feeling a touch punch drunk at all this and at the same time strangely enough fancies a drink.

'Go on.'

'Well, then there are the hormones.'

Conway is back in full flow now and has even speeded up a bit.

'Testosterone, adrenaline, I could go on. We also mustn't forget that all these things may be magnified by the 'disability' factor.'

Conway does that finger quotation in the air – something that always annoys Milan.

'Because she is cut off from certain other stimuli she may be hyper aware of the ones that she is getting, for example the ones from your blood chemistry that I mentioned.'

'Do you mean like a blind piano tuner having extra sensitive hearing?'

Conway nods.

'There is quite a difference of opinion if that is in fact the case regarding the blind piano tuners, but that's the kind of thing I'm talking about.'

She seems to have come to the end of her list.

She sits back looking suddenly rather tired. Milan has a brief image of Conway conversing with Dr Snell and the disparity between their speeds of communication.

He feels flooded with information but at the same time Conway hasn't in any way answered the question that has been on his mind all weekend.

'But what does she think about? What's been going through her head all this time?'

Conway holds her hands up, palms forward.

'Wait a minute, that's completely out of our depth at the minute. She has lived for forty-two years with only sound and chemicals for company. She might be unable to develop cognitive processes that we could recognise. She may even have made up her own world. She has no language presumably, so what must that mean to the way she structures her world? We think in words after all. Without language certain people even question whether thought as we know it is possible.'

Milan is looking somewhat depressed by all this. Conway surprisingly claps her hands, once, quite loudly. Milan is not sure if this is a trick of her trade or just an idiosyncrasy of hers. It makes him jump anyway.

'There is a very simple way to answer your question. Ask her what she thinks. Teach her how to speak and then ask her. Get her to write her autobiography, even. I'd read it.'

Conway leans back again in her chair; she seems to have bursts of energy that then tire her out. In any case she has hit the ball squarely into his court.

'OK. Where do I start?'

'You are in rather a unique situation. My two best bets would be people who are looking after patients who are in long term comas or, more promisingly, those involved in teaching the vocally, aurally and visually challenged.'

There is a knock at the door. A couple of students look

in. The professor asks them to give her five minutes. They nod and go away again.

'There was the famous Helen Keller of course. Maybe you could read up on her. But, I don't think we can forget that Roma's actual communication difficulties are significantly magnified even compared to her. This is not going to be easy. However, you have to start somewhere.'

She writes something down for him.

'Here is an address in London. A small specialised school. Tell them I recommended you.'

As Milan leaves he promises to keep the professor up with any developments.

She stops him in the doorway.

'One last thing. You are filling her full of your hormones and adrenaline; my guess is that she might be contributing some of those to your joint blood stream.'

'No man is an island?'

'Especially in your case.'

Outside her office Milan has to sit down. The students waiting look at him curiously. His legs are weak. Time for that drink he thinks.

At the HK teaching centre they are at first extremely suspicious of him. Milan is trying to explain as much of his situation as possible without adding fuel to the publicity bonfire. Finally he mentions the professor and everything changes. He is advised that a certain Ms Khambaty is the ultimate multiple-disabilities teacher. He tracks her down in one of the teaching rooms.

Milan had expected to find someone older but she is very young. She is in her early twenties, maybe, with several piercings including her nose and quite a punky outfit, with a short black skirt over trousers. She has a child of about three on her lap who does not move all the time Milan is there, but stares into space. Ms Khambaty continuously taps the child's hand.

Milan decides to be open with her and explain the entire situation concerning Roma. Ms Khambaty asks to touch his back where the tapping is centred, but all is quiet.

Milan confesses to her his uncertainty over what to do.

'I haven't a clue how to begin with all this. I read that Müller book about Helen Keller, you know, that tells you how her teacher broke through to her by pouring water on her hands, but it doesn't seem relevant. Helen Keller had already had experiences before she lost her sight and hearing. But Roma never has, so where do I start? Also, I can't stick Roma's hand under a water tap, can I?'

Ms Khambaty listens to his tirade and nods. She sucks some air in between her teeth. She has a tiny gap between her front two which is strangely attractive. At last she speaks.

'You've got to get into her world somehow. She doesn't have the possibility of experiencing water but she must have something equivalent. She is alive after all, so she she must be experiencing things. All you have to do is name those experiences. The first thing you must do is instil in her the idea that communication is a possibility, that the tapping she makes can mean something other than itself.'

She pauses for a few minutes.

Milan sits and waits.

'What does Roma experience?' she asks at last.

Milan's agitation is subsiding. He realises that he has been in a state for the last three days since he saw the professor. But Ms Khambaty is very calming. Perhaps it is because she is completely used to not being rushed, taking time, having to take time.

'The main thing that I know she experiences is, I suppose, music.'

Ms Khambaty nods.

'OK then, we start with music. You play her a tune. Then you name it. You play it again; then you name it again. Give her time to let it sink in. If she ever comes up with the name then you must play the piece to reinforce the idea. Once one name is established then you play another tune. Give it its own unique name. Use one of the existing tapping systems if you want to or make up you own.'

'But the people you are dealing with can't hear; Roma can, after all. In a way I could speak to her in normal language. Teach her what words mean.'

Ms Khambaty nods again.

'You could certainly do that – but the problem you

would have to face is that she can't communicate back to you that same way. You have no feedback device to let you know if she is learning things; you don't know when to move on from one thing to the next, from one word to another. Also she would have to use a different system to talk to you; she has no way of speaking after all.'

She shrugs.

'I definitely think you must start with a basic tapping symbol system. You can't use this one, the one that I am using here, because it has spatial elements and you don't have the possibility of that. What you need is more a kind of Morse code maybe. Later on when progress is being made you could introduce spoken words as a sort of bilingual language.'

'You mean normal Morse code, like *dot dot dash*, that kind of thing?'

'Why not just stick with that exactly? There is no point in reinventing the wheel after all. Use stress for the difference between the dots and dashes. Can Roma make different emphases in her tapping?'

Milan feels his back sympathetically.

'Yes, she has quite a dynamic range.'

'Another problem is making your tapping audible to her. I guess she is tapping on bone?'

'It certainly feels like it.'

'Just tapping on your hip or something probably won't have enough definition.'

Milan tells her of Roma and him duetting with the *William Tell Overture*, but she is not impressed.

'That kind of musical stuff can afford to be somewhat vague. With words you need precision. Give me a minute.'

She thinks for a while. He looks around. The place is very light and airy with a lot of pictures on the walls.

'This might sound a bit weird but I think it could work. Put a piece of metal on a belt around your waist and get a couple of metal thimbles to tap it with. That should give you enough definition to talk to her.'

After all Milan has been through he would have thought nothing would surprise him but somehow this young woman advising him to tap with metal thimbles on a belt-thing nearly makes him laugh out loud.

'A belt, with a metal bit on it, and two thimbles?'

She nods. She is nearly laughing herself.

'Give it a go.'

Milan notices that the child who he thought was immobile has occasionally been tapping his teacher's hand back.

Ms Khambaty translates for him.

'He likes you.'

'But he can't see or hear me; how does he even know I'm here?'

'I told him you'd come in, what you were like. What your problem was, what you were trying to do.'

The child reaches out his hand. Milan shakes it solemnly. He feels a tiny tapping from it. Like a bird.

'He said come again,' she translates. Milan feels his interview is over.

He moves to the door.

'Tell him I will.'

She waves sweetly as Milan goes and then turns her attention back to the child.

That evening Milan is meant to be going to one of Karen's concerts but he can't wait to try out his first experiment. When he phones Karen to tell her he is not coming she sounds a bit put out but he thinks he can make it up to her.

He has bought a small portable cassette player. He also has a Morse code book he found at a scout shop on his way home. His mission to find two metal thimbles was completely unsuccessful, however. Half a dozen shop-people have looked at him as if he was a bit of a sad case.

'Thimbles?'

'Yes, you know, you use them for darning things, don't you?'

'Darning? Do people still do darning?'

Apparently not. Milan expects they just buy new things and throw away their socks with holes in them. Anyway, for this evening he has decided to try improvising with two dessert spoons. Trying to manipulate them, read the book and work the cassette player all at the same time, he realises the subtlety of Ms Khambaty's solution.

Milan decides to start with Beethoven's fifth symphony. You could say it's their song after all. At last he gets everything in place to start and taps out in Morse code:

< Beethoven Fifth >

Then he plays the opening of the symphony on the cassette. Then he does both again, then again, then again. Then he waits. He gets himself a beer. He starts again. He is wishing that he had chosen a piece of music that he wasn't so familiar with.

An hour and a half later, just as Milan is beginning to wonder if maybe his sister is as sick of this piece as he is and knows how to say its name, but is keeping quiet because she doesn't actually want to hear it again, he feels a tentative < Beethoven Fifth > being tapped from inside him. In his excitement he can hardly start the cassette player. At last he gets it going. As soon as he stops it he gets the same message.

< Beethoven Fifth > Over and over it comes, just like a child saying *again*, *again*, *again*. Each time Roma asks for it Milan plays it for her, the first two or three minutes of the symphony. He can't believe that she really wants to hear that piece so many times. He thinks it must be the sheer pleasure of asking for something and receiving it that is delighting her so much. However, after seven or eight times he himself wants a change.

Milan decides to try the Mozart clarinet concerto next.

He taps in:

< Mozart Clar Conc Slow > and plays the start of the middle movement.

Two minutes later it comes back:

< Mozart Clar Conc Slow >

My little sister is no dummy, Milan thinks to himself. While the concerto is playing for the third time he gets to wondering whether she is in fact his little sister? Littler in size of course, not younger, but definitely littler.

By the end of the evening she has learnt the names of thirty-four compositions and Milan is struggling to remember them all himself, even with them written in his notebook and with the huge pile of cassettes to remind him. Reinforcement, reinforcement, reinforcement Ms Khambaty had insisted. Once you start you have to keep it up.

He decides, however, that enough is enough. He needs a negative command. He taps in:

< No >

He gets back:

< Mozart Thirty Two >

He doesn't play it but taps:

< No >

After ten or more tries eventually she stops.

Milan feels equally exulted and exhausted.

That night Milan can't sleep for planning. He needs a *yes* to go with the *no*. In the morning when she asks for a piece of music he taps:

< Yes > after her requests and then plays them.

By lunchtime he thinks Roma now has a *yes* and a *no* in her vocabulary.

Roma demands Sibelius; Milan says < No >

She says < Yes >

He says < No >

She says < Yes >

< Yes >

< No >

< Yes >

< No >

In the end he gives in. For the second time he is reminded of a child.

Karen rings in the afternoon. They had arranged to meet that morning for her to show him a new concert dress she was thinking of buying. He has compounded the sin of the previous evening. In his excitement over his progress with Roma he can't take Karen's complaints about looking for a dress seriously. She, however, remains resolutely unimpressed with everything he tells her about the communications progress with Roma.

'Maybe you could try communicating with me sometime,' she remarks rather acidly.

A couple of days later Milan goes back to the centre to see Ms Khambaty. This time she has no child with her but is filling in forms at a desk – she does not look so happy as before.

'So, what advances have we made?' she asks immediately. She beckons him to sit down.

'Well we've – and I mean we, this is as much hard work for me – we've learnt the names for seventy-eight pieces of music and I think a sort of a *yes* and a sort of a *no*. I'm using a kind of Morse code language like you suggested. Actually it is Morse code more or less.'

Ms Khambaty comes round from her desk.

'Show me how you are doing it?'

Milan has brought with him the cassette player and a pile of cassettes.

He taps out the code for *Rhapsody in Blue* on a coin he has glued to a belt just over his hipbone with his brand new thimbles. He has placed Ms Khambaty's hand on the small of his back. It feels like rather a delicate moment for him. She however seems totally unperturbed – it's what she does after all. Her hand feels warm through his shirt.

A reply comes from Roma. She smiles.

'That's a *no* isn't it?'

'That is a *no*, three times *no*, actually.' Milan knew it would be; he had chosen that piece deliberately to get a *no*.

'Wait, she is saying something else now.'

< Mahler – nine – fourth – movement >

Miss Khambaty is slightly struggling with straightforward Morse code but she comes up with it. It feels to Milan that his sister is the most expert of the three of them in that language. He is still at the stage of looking through notes and his scout book for every other word.

'I haven't got that Mahler with me. Two can say no.'

Milan taps the:

< No >

They get more tapping.

'Now she wants Bach, Brandenburg Four, first movement, which we do actually have. So that's a *yes*.'

He puts on the cassette after tapping the *yes* and puts the player in his back pocket playing softly. They both, Ms Khambaty and him, listen as well for a while.

'The problem for me is where do we go from here? We could just go on learning thousands of pieces of music but it doesn't seem to be leading anywhere. It feels like a kind of Pavlov's dog thing.'

Ms Khambaty is smiling and shaking her head in disbelief.

'You are crazy. You should be out celebrating. I can't believe how easily you have made this first jump. It's incredible. I thought it would take you months; she is a little brain-box your sister. Now that the concept of naming things is established the sky is the limit. Nouns, verbs, adjectives – anything she can experience you can get through to her as a symbol. Then you're into abstract thoughts, philosophy, religion. You'll be amazed at what is possible. Just start slowly and then after a while branch out.'

She sits back down at her desk slightly embarrassed by her overt display of enthusiasm.

She takes a deep breath.

'What else can she experience apart from music?'

Milan gets out the list he made after visiting Professor Conway.

'Other sounds, blood sugar, blood contents, movement.'

She thinks a moment.

'OK, this is the plan. Every time you are going to do anything then give her the word for it first. You want to drink a cup of coffee, give her the word *coffee*, you are going for a run, give her the word *run*, lying down, word, bath, word, cigarette, word. Don't even think whether it is something she can experience or understand or anything, just do it automatically.'

'I gave up – cigarettes I mean.'

'You gave them up, did you, but did she?'

The cassette has stopped.

'But all those words won't mean the same to her as to me, if I run she's not running.'

'The important thing is consistency. She's not running but experiencing something particular as you run. Worry about the details later.'

Something in her passion for all this stirs Milan.

'How did you get to be so wise at such a tender age?'

Even as Milan says this he feels he is being slightly patronising to her.

Ms Khambaty is not patronised however.

'I spend a lot of time listening – and not just with my ears.'

Milan tries running on his way home. First he taps the word < Run > and then sprints a hundred yards. The third time he tries it he gets back a < No. No. Nononono >. He sits down quite puffed in any case; the only exercise he gets these days is with his bowing arm.

Tentatively Milan taps out < Cigarette > and cautiously lights one. As soon as he left the teaching centre he went into the first newsagents he came to. His conquered addiction needed only the tiniest green light, the smallest excuse to re-establish itself. The running has opened his lungs and the smoke stings abrasively. That deep subtle sense of relief floods him. How long is it since his last one, two years at least? Someone else has been missing the cigarettes these last years: all the way home the tapping is incessant.

< Cigarette, yes, cigarette, yes, cigarette, yes >

Thank God four-year-olds aren't allowed to smoke Milan thinks – we'd never hear the end of it and the screaming in supermarket queues would be incessant.

5

Two weeks later after much progress with Roma's vocabulary Karen and Milan arrive for dinner at Andreas's place. Andreas is cooking. His oldest daughter lets them in. She is called Marta and is around fourteen. She hangs up their coats and then takes them through to the kitchen. Andreas is wearing a butcher's pinafore with fake blood stains down the front.

'Anjy, Karen – Karen, Anjy.'

Milan can see Andreas comparing her to his description. Milan was fairly conservative in describing her charms and she is wearing one of her nicest black dresses. Milan interrupts before Karen notices Andreas's attention.

'Can I smoke?'

Karen is shaking her head ruefully. She has refused to kiss him since Milan started again.

'It such a trick,' she says. 'They put cigarettes in nice little clean box, all wrapped up with cellophane, and they look so neat and clean and white in their little box but then when you look in old stinky ashtray you see what they really like.'

'Well,' Milan retorts, 'you could say humans look all nice and clean wrapped up in their clothes and skin, but if you look in their coffins, then they don't look so nice.'

'In your coffin, that where you end up with your smoking,' she whips back at him.

Milan feels he asked for that one.

Andreas joins Karen in her disapproval.

'You gave up years ago?'

'I know, I know, but it's not for me,' Milan says before Marta comes back in and joins the anti-smoking brigade.

He points at his stomach.

'I'll get no peace all evening if I don't have one. Click click all night you know. The taxi had a *no smoking* notice in it, otherwise I would have got it over with before we got here.'

Actually Milan is being ordered to smoke by two masters. His own cravings and Roma's have formed an unholy alliance. She seems to embody desire without any of the normal restraints, either moral or health-wise. Milan thinks one of the next phrases she should learn ought to be cancer, of the lung variety.

Andreas relents.

'If you have to, you have to. Just open the back door and lean out. I want to make it to fifty, you know.'

All the time they are talking Milan is looking around the kitchen. Andreas has this trick of rearranging objects and suchlike – pictures, glasses, whatever, so that the total makes up an image.

Marta comes back in to the kitchen and says, 'Did they see the elephant, Dad?'

Andreas shakes his head and pretends he is going to throw an onion at her.

'Bigmouth.'

Marta withdraws behind the door momentarily.

'Ooops.'

Now that she has mentioned it Milan can see the elephant easily. Once you have it, the more you look the clearer it gets. Karen is still looking around, although Milan had already briefed her on the concept before they got there.

'OK, elephant? Where?' Nobody fills her in.

Milan lights up his cigarette. It is an extra mild one.

Milan taps out:

< Cigarette coming >

< Shit cigarette or excellent cigarette? >

< Shit cigarette > Milan answers truthfully. Roma can calculate the nicotine content to a fraction of a percent on just the first two puffs. Capstan Full Strength would probably be her idea of heaven. Anyway, extra light is all she's getting tonight; if she wants something else let her buy it herself.

Milan leans out of the door and blows the smoke into the cold night air.

'Winter is on its way,' he announces back to the three of them as if he had just got a psychic premonition, rather than stating the obvious.

'It soon be Christmas,' follows up Karen.

'What kind of present do you think I should get for Roma? What do you get for the girl who has nothing?'

Andreas uses a wooden spoon as a microphone.

'Imagine no possessions, it's easy if you try-y.'

Whoever gave him the impression that he can sing, Milan wonders.

'Daaad,' complains Marta; obviously it wasn't her.

'Of course I could get her a new CD of one of her favourite pieces.'

'More important what you get for me,' says Karen, sounding slightly piqued.

Andreas is frying his onions now.

'I had a great idea. You can use the musical stuff to teach Roma other words.'

'Such as?'

'Such as *up* and *down*.'

'What? You mean like, play a scale going up and tell her that is *up*. Then get up and tell her that is *up* as well, kind of thing?'

Andreas nods.

Milan has already thought of that idea.

'The problem with that is no one is quite sure why up in music is *up*. It could just as easy be the other way. You know, like Australia being at the top of the world and not the bottom.'

'But up is up. One note is higher than another.'

'It could just be cultural thing, something you learn. Also me getting up is that up for Roma?'

'Or you could go up in a lift. Anyway, none of that matters.'

Andreas is getting excited now.

'Even if she gets it the other way round she *is* getting it. Say I had taught Marta that green was called *blue* when she was little...'

Marta is now chopping peppers but listening.

'Thanks Dad.'

'She would still know what *blue* was to her.'

'I would have had a dorky time at school with the other kids.'

'A rose by any other name.'

Milan agrees to give it a try just to keep Andreas quiet.

Marta carries on chopping but gives Milan sneaky glances, especially at his stomach.

'Want to take a photo?' he asks her.

'Sorry,' she says blushing.

Milan immediately feels bad about embarrassing her.

'I keep expecting her to pop out like in that *Alien* film,' Marta continues.

'Or like that small man sticking out in *Total Recall*,' joins in Andreas.

Karen even comes up with, 'Has anybody seen *Men in Black* with the tiny guy controlling...'

'Enough!' Milan stops them all, 'she is staying put.'

Dinner is eventually served.

They all sit round for the first course which is inevitably Andreas's beetroot borscht.

Andreas puts what can only be described as a cauldron down in the middle of the table.

'Do you know what the secret of good borscht is?' he asks them all.

Milan and Marta chorus in unison, 'When it is done strain it and then add a ton of sugar.'

'Exactly.'

He ladles it out.

It is extremely sweet. Milan personally does not like the mixing up of savoury and sweet courses. He cannot stand Chinese sweet and sour; it just tastes like sweet vinegar to him. Roma on the other hand will be extremely partial to this borscht. Milan makes a note to explain to her later the concept of the sugar crash when the insulin in his body, or rather their body – in a way it is as much hers as his – when the insulin will swill around their blood sucking up the sugar molecules and depressing them endlessly until they get hold of another sugar hit from somewhere.

Hold on a minute, it's not so long since she learned yes and no and now Milan is thinking how he is going to teach her the word insulin. Well Ms Khambaty said the sky was the limit.

With the arrival of a pile of filo pastries the conversation turns to time.

Andreas starts it with, 'It's already been at least a month since you discovered Roma, hasn't it?'

'Or rather since she discovered me,' Milan replies. 'But it only seems like yesterday.'

'Time seems to be speeding up faster and faster if you ask me,' Andreas carries on cryptically.

'I have theory about time,' interjects Karen.

'I too have a time theory,' this is Andreas again.

Marta chimes in with,

'I don't have a theory but a funny saying about time.'

Milan decides to take charge.

'OK, we hear Andreas's theory first, then Karen's and then Marta's saying.'

'Why Andreas before me?' complains Karen.

'Age before beauty,' Milan tells her.

'There's no arguing with that in this case,' Marta chimes in, getting a stern look from her father.

'Carry on then,' accepts Karen.

Andreas puffs himself up and actually stands to deliver his oratory.

'My theory is that when we are young everything is new to us. As we get older we are increasingly doing things, experiencing situations, you know, that we have already encountered. Therefore there is less novelty in our lives and we measure time by the amount of novelty.' He sits back down adding a concluding, 'Amen.'

Milan nods sagely, and then to Karen. She doesn't stand

up but clears her throat importantly before beginning.

'My theory is that more you enjoy yourself then more quickly time passes. Therefore more bored you are…'

'Such as sitting in a boring classroom,' butts in Marta.

Karen nods.

'Exactly, more slowly time pass. As we get older we get more control and can therefore steer our lives into more enjoyable areas and so time pass faster.'

In his role as adjudicator, or maybe it should be ringmaster, Milan decides to take the coward's way out.

'What would therefore happen if we later in life encounter something new that is at the same time extremely pleasurable?' This does everybody's head in.

Karen saves the day by saying, 'Marta, we forget your funny saying.'

Marta, like her father, stands up.

'Time flies like an arrow; fruit flies like a banana.'

They all nod.

'Did you make that up?' Milan asks her impressed.

'No, it was Groucho Marx,' she answers.

'Ah, Gloucho,' Karen repeats with what Milan is sure is a deliberate *el*.

Everybody laughs.

At the end of the meal Karen states emphatically, patting her tummy, 'That was most delicious meal.'

Marta observes,

'You never say *the*, I mean the word *the* do you?'

'We don' have word *the* in Japanese.'

'Why not? How can you manage without *the*-s? We're always using them,' carries on Marta.

'*The* complete waste of time, if you ask me.'

Andreas butts in now.

'But when you say *the* it's different from *a*.'

'OK, you say *a man* comes down street, or you say *the man* comes down street, still *man* coming down street whatever.'

Marta is back in the fray.

'But *a man* is not the same as *the man*.'

'Both have two legs and head,' rejoins Karen enigmatically.

After much heated debate it is finally agreed that there is a difference between *a man* and *the man*, but not one to warrant littering up our language with barrow-loads of *the*-s and *a*-s, not to mention all that ink that gets used up, when in the tiny percent of cases where it does make a difference you could just say *that man*, or even use his name.

On the walk home, however, Karen doesn't seem so happy.

'Do you really have to do that tapping whole evening?'

Milan doesn't live far from Andreas and Karen has reluctantly agreed to stay at his place.

'I was only keeping Roma up to date with what was being said. I thought I was doing it pretty quietly.'

'It's not noise; it just looks fidgety and you don' seem to be paying attention to what's going on around, especially to me.'

Milan feels himself starting to get a bit cross. They are both tired and have drunk too much.

'I think it's a bit selfish to just…' Milan realises this is the wrong thing to say as soon as he says it.

Karen has stopped half-way across a road.

'Selfish? You think it selfish to go out with somebody an' want them to spend just little attention on you?'

Cars are swerving around them; one hoots his horn. Time to back down, Milan thinks.

'I'm sorry, I didn't mean to say that. Let's get off the road.'

Back on the pavement Milan continues.

'Look, it's hard for me just now with all this going on. I promise that I will be more thoughtful in future.'

Even as Milan is saying this he can feel Roma asking for a cigarette. Milan decides to ignore her.

Karen grudgingly accepts his apology and they head home. Milan thinks she may even be crying. He tries to put his arm round her shoulder but she merely shrugs it off.

Milan goes back to the centre for the third time.

This time Ms Khambaty has three children with her. They are playing with a construction set. They are feeling for the pieces and snapping them together. Frequently they are tapping each other's hands or arms or whatever. They are laughing, sometimes very loudly.

Ms Khambaty stands up and kisses Milan on the cheek.

'We've got to stop meeting like this,' she laughs.

Milan is taken aback with the kiss.

'I'm sorry to keep bothering you.'

'No, no, keep coming back, I'm completely fascinated by all this. Where are we up to now?'

'I've expanded into using other words. *Run* seems to work, *cigarette* has been a big hit, but I'm kind of stuck again.'

Ms Khambaty nods.

'The answer is to cram her full of information. Don't even think about it; just give her the words. Let her make her own sense of them. When a baby learns you just talk to it, you don't try to teach it to speak. Some of it goes in, some doesn't; it's volume that counts. You take a child for a walk, you see a dog, you say *dog*. You don't worry if the child might think *dog* means brown or dangerous. You see a fire you say *hot*, or you say *fire* or you say *red*. None of it matters. The child sees a red ball, a red jacket, a red fire, a red apple and in the end the concept of *red* seeps in. She sees a blue ball, a white ball and so on and then the word *ball* seeps in. One day you show her an orange ball she has never seen before and she says *orange ball* all by herself.'

'Maybe I'm panicking, do you think? As if I have to catch up, you know, forty-two years.'

'You have all the time in the world,' she answers him. It sounds like a quote from something but Milan can't place it.

Milan has made a list of words he thinks Roma knows. He gets it out and passes it over and she reads it aloud slowly and deliberately.

'*Roma, I, morning, afternoon, sleep*, all the music pitches, all the music durations, *fast, slow, medium, chocolate, beer, wine, hangover, up, down, run, walk, bath, shit* (as in not good), *excellent, borscht, yes, no*, some hundred and twenty musical compositions, *Beethoven, Bach, modern music, violin, trumpet, synthesiser*, seventeen other instruments, *happy, sad, please* (not sure about that one), numbers up to ninety-nine (got bored with that game), *beautiful, ugly, rain* (her favourite word, always asked for).'

Ms Khambaty laughs when she gets to *rain*.

'Rain must just be a pleasant noise for her tucked up snug and warm with no worries. What a world she must live in. I sometimes wonder about these ones here,' she ruffles the hair of one of the girls who immediately smiles, 'But even they have a wealth of experiences and relationships compared to your Roma.'

'Imagine never just holding something in your hands.'

'Or someone,' Ms Khambaty says. For the second time in the afternoon Milan feels a certain warmth from her.

He puts that out of his mind.

'I just can't get it, what it must be like being her, that's the problem.'

'The reason you can't get it is because all you can imagine is you, yourself, in her situation, having had all the experiences you've had. It's the same with these children, you have to just let go of your own world and enter theirs afresh, in a state of innocence.'

'It feels like she's a little Robinson Crusoe, and I'm her island.'

Ms Khambaty takes his hand.

'You're not the island; you're the ship that's come to take her home.'

6

MILAN's cousin Ella has turned up. She is a bossy forty-eight-year-old. Somehow those extra years older as a child seem to stick with you. When you are five years old a ten-year-old is a god who knows everything and has such powers and control over you. When you are fifty, on the other hand, a fifty-five-year-old is your equal, but if you knew each other as children those memories linger in both parties. Having heard about Milan's problem, she has come to look after him. Thanks, he thinks.

She has brought a bottle of gin and two large bottles of tonic. Milan never usually drinks gin and tonic but it seems to go down well. Milan gets the thumbs up from down below, anyway.

Ella cooks him his dinner; it's cauliflower cheese.

The two sit down at the table.

Ella has been fairly subdued all through the greetings and the cooking but suddenly bursts out with, 'I think it's a nightmare scenario. It's trapped like a prisoner.'

'By *it* you mean Roma?' and then Milan adds for effect,

'Your *cousin* Roma.'

Milan thinks the *cousin* startles her but she carries on.

'In any case, this Roma can't move, can't see. Imagine if a prisoner were treated like that; what a fuss your Amnesty would make.'

My Amnesty? Milan thinks momentarily.

He takes up the gauntlet anyhow.

'How can you be a prisoner from something you don't know exists? You can't miss the outside, or movement, if you've never experienced it.'

Milan sees from Ella's eyes that he has left a flaw in his argument and waits for the riposte. She takes her time. Helps herself to more cauliflower. Milan waits for the verbal blow. Here it comes.

'OK then, Milo, what about a battery chicken? It's never seen outside or felt the wind and all that, but you can't tell me that it's not deprived. It's a genetic thing; it misses them anyway.'

Milan is stumped for an answer. Part of him thinks she is a bit right. She is on a roll now and carries on.

'Say someone had a child and kept it in a black room for ten years and then got taken to court for cruelty. And she said *but Your Honour,*' Ella puts on her whining liberal type voice for this sentence, '*my child never suffered because she never knew the outside so how could she miss it*? I don't think she would be walking out the door with just a fine, do you?'

Ella sits back in her chair triumphant.

All Milan can think to answer is a pathetic, 'This is different.'

Ella carries on.

'She's living like one of those vegetable people, like those lying paralysed in a hospital, unable to move or see. What kind of a life is that?'

'She's conscious, she's aware – she's happy.' Is Milan trying to convince his cousin or himself?

'How do you really know that? With your tippertytappty?'

'Ask her.'

Milan suddenly feels slightly afraid. Not of the question itself, but more to do with how Roma will deal with another person speaking to her. How can Milan indicate that a different person is communicating with her?

Ella however is keen to try it. Milan shows her the tapping signs for *Roma*, *is*, *happy* and *yes*.

She practices a few times with the thimbles on the table. Then she taps his belt. Milan places her hand on the small of his back and she feels the vivid response.

'That wasn't *yes*,' Ella declares, 'What was that?'

'That was *no, Roma is sad*,' Milan admits. 'Nobody is happy all the time.'

Ella however seems to have been somewhat touched by the unexpected response. And after a thoughtful few minutes she asks him to find out why Roma – she even uses her proper name now – is sad. After a few complicated exchanges Milan declares, 'I don't think she knows why.'

Ella shifts the conversation.

'Where's your other new friend, the Japanese one?'

'Her name is Karen.' Ella seems to be deliberately not using people's names at the minute. 'We're not getting on too well these days.'

'Musical differences?'

'What do you mean?'

'She's musical and you're different.'

The gin seems to be working on Ella.

'That was a kind of joke, was it?'

She smiles.

'Sort of. Anyway, what is the reason?'

'A lot of it seems to revolve around Roma.'

'The old green-eyed goddess?'

Milan doesn't know where she gets these phrases. Maybe his cousin should team up with Andreas, and do a double act.

'It's not exactly jealousy. It's based on fact. I am distracted a lot of the time. I should pay more attention to Karen, but I feel responsible to Roma. I am her eyes after all.'

Ella shrugs.

'I seem to be getting your full and undivided attention at the minute.'

Milan picks up the gin bottle to pour them both another.

'Thanks to this you are. She's practically asleep.'

Ella stays the night on Milan's sofa bed. In the morning all three of them have hangovers. All three of them have aspirin and strong coffee and two of them eat chocolate (you can work it out yourselves). Two of them feel a lot better; the third gets the train back to Reigate.

On Ella's departure Roma announces < I like our cousin > although Milan is not sure if it is Ella's personality she likes or the bottle of gin she brought.

Milan personally resolves to stick to wine and beer for the time being, for both of their sakes.

Roma has a new game.

She has tapped out an < E >

Milan is at a bit of a loss.

There it is again.

Eventually the penny drops and Milan pick up his violin and plays an E.

Roma taps a < C >

Milan plays a C.

Then a < D >

Milan plays a D.

Milan gets a < Down >

Milan plays the D an octave lower. Soon Milan has a row of twenty-odd notes. Roma taps the whole lot together but in rhythm. Milan plays the melody. She taps:

< Fast >

Milan plays it faster.

< Fast >

Milan plays it even faster.

Milan hears a < Yes > tapped.

Milan writes it down on a piece of manuscript. At the top Milan writes 'Roma Kotzia' where the composer's name might go. It is not the most brilliant tune in the world but Milan has certainly never heard it before.

It is the week before Christmas and Karen and Milan have made up again. Milan has promised to devote himself to her when she is with him and she is going to learn to talk to Roma. She comes round to cook a special three-month anniversary meal for him. Milan has spent several hours tidying and cleaning the flat. It is certainly nowhere near her standard but she seems impressed that he has made a bit of an effort. She makes his favourite noodles with some strange mushrooms.

They have wine with the meal, nearly two bottles in fact. Afterwards they listen to music, Karen's choice of Mendelssohn, despite vague protests from below. Milan puts his arm around Karen on the sofa. He slips his hand under her blouse. He kisses her wine-flavoured lips. They move onto the floor and he pulls her tights down. He slips into her. He forgets himself in her.

A few minutes later he feels a sudden emphatic tapping.

< Stop >

It is unmistakable. Someone down there is not happy. Milan decides to ignore it in view of his recent promises to Karen.

Roma keeps going.

< Stop, stop, stop, stop >

Milan pulls out. And lies still. The tapping has ceased abruptly.

'What is it?'

Karen looks at him concerned.

'She told me to stop,' Milan tells her.

There is an incredulous pause. And then, 'Roma? You mean, Roma told you stop, don' you? Who she? Your mummy?'

Milan tries to explain but feels he's just getting into even deeper water.

'It's not a moral thing with Roma. It's not even a jealous thing; she doesn't even know if other people exist as far as I'm aware.'

'And?'

'Well it's probably a motion thing that's upsetting her.'

All of a sudden Karen is doing up her blouse. Her lips have a certain firmness. She stands up.

'I suggest you sort things out with that little madam and then you ring me.'

She leaves without another word.

Milan remains seated on the floor strangely paralysed.

Three's a crowd he thinks softly.

He feels a familiar tapping. It's a request, for a cigarette.

Milan thinks he must work more on the *please* concept. He lights up the cigarette with a certain sense of irony. They both settle down to enjoy the substances flooding their bloodstream.

Next morning Milan goes to see Ms Khambaty. She is back with the child Milan originally saw her with. She seems surprised but not displeased with this unexpected visit. The child's name is Danny. Danny spells it out for Milan on his hand.

'What's the latest progress with our Roma?' she asks.

'For a start, she's managed to split me up with my girlfriend.'

Ms Khambaty opens her eyes wide.

'I'm impressed, the minx. What strategy did she use?'

'She told me to stop having sex with her.'

'And you listened?' She is trying to suppress a smile.

'She has got my spine in her sticky little paw.'

'That's true enough. Was she jealous, then?'

'I think it's more of a movement thing that she didn't like. It probably gave her a headache.'

Ms Khambaty is busily tapping on Danny's hand all this time.

'You're not telling him all this, are you?' Milan asks, slightly alarmed.

'No, no, no. He just asked me what you were wearing. Anyway, how did your girlfriend react?'

'She stormed out in a fury.'

Ms Khambaty nods thoughtfully.

'Maybe she'll be back?'

Milan feels himself sighing, from weariness?

'I doubt it; it's a long story.'

'Anyway it was a silly thing for her to do. She should just have gone on top.'

Ms Khambaty's eyes have a flash of something.

'Is that a come on?'

She smiles properly this time.

'Do you want it to be?' She is tapping continuously to Danny. Milan is impressed how she can maintain two conversations at once; it must be something like the way a translator simultaneously listens and talks. It's a skill Milan needed with Karen he thinks belatedly.

Milan is suddenly feeling reckless.

'When do you finish work?'

'Six.'

'I'll be back then, then.'

'I'll see you then, then.'

Milan takes Ms Khambaty to the pub, or rather she takes him, on the back of her scooter. She has only one helmet with her and insists Milan wears it. He has never been so scared in his life as she squeezes them between buses and lorries. While she drives, or is it scoots, she shouts at him over her shoulder that her first name is Murri. She already knows his.

'Are you named after that *lightness-of-being* chap?'

They are going surprisingly fast for London with all this zigzagging and a certain disregard for traffic lights and Milan finds it difficult to talk.

'Milan Kundera, you mean? No, my parents just liked pizza. You read the book?'

Milan wishes she would concentrate on the road and realises he is holding her quite tightly round the waist out of fear and panic although it feels pleasantly intimate as well.

'No, but I saw the film.'

She parks near her place in Camden and they walk the rest of the way. Milan is extremely glad to be back on dry land. Out in the streets and in her denim jacket she looks punkier than ever.

The bar is full and they have to stand with their drinks.

Milan shows her a new list, words Milan thinks Roma will never know: *star, blue, cloud, sycamore tree, full moon, mother, face, grass, book, electricity, love.*

Murri is as ever philosophical and positive.

'Think of each of the words as a gift. Each one is a bonus.'

'My cup is half-full stuff?'

'If you like. Plus doesn't this make you think how lucky you are yourself? You've got the whole lot of them. Hundreds of thousands of them.'

Milan nods wisely.

She carries on.

'Anyway, give me your list. This word we can do.' She scores the words out with a short stub of a pencil. '...and this...and this, this, this mmm? Maybe this...and this.'

Milan looks at the list with words scratched out. She has only left *blue*.

'Giving up on *blue*? It's not like you to be so negative?' Milan chides her.

'Oh, what the hell.'

Murri strikes out the word *blue* as well.

Milan gets them another round of drinks to celebrate.

Murri has gone on top. There has been satisfaction all round, three orgasms for the price of two.

She is now singing softly next to him tucked in under his arm. Milan pulls the duvet up over them.

'There was three in the bed,
and the little one said,
roll over,
roll over.'

She is tapping away all the time the words to the song on his hip. She has a way of clicking her fingers so she doesn't need the thimbles. It seems to work for Roma.

'So they all rolled over,
and one fell out,
there was two in the bed.'

Milan feels a twinge of conscience over Karen. Surely

Murri is referring to him and her and Roma as the three, or maybe not?

Milan decides to join in anyway.

'And the little one said,

roll over,

roll over.'

Next morning around seven Milan slowly wakes up. There is tapping to the left of him, tapping to the right.

'What's going on?'

Murri is lying close to him; she has put on one of his shirts.

'We didn't want to waken you.'

'What are you two going on about?'

'Oh, it's just girl's talk, that's all.'

'Carry on then; it's just my body after all.'

Milan closes his eyes but doesn't go back to sleep. He lies there enjoying the to-ing and fro-ing. This could be the start of a beautiful friendship, he thinks.

That morning Milan goes out leaving Murri in his flat. Milan has a few Saturday morning lessons to give, the last before Christmas. Three or four hours later he comes back and the flat is spotless.

Murri is now washing the inside of the windows for the first time in years.

His flat is in a state of shock.

'Some Japanese woman came round,' Murri tells him.

'She let herself in. I was up to my arms in washing-up and didn't hear her. I nearly jumped out of my skin.'

Some Japanese woman? Murri knows perfectly well it was Karen.

'That must have been a surprise for her too, seeing you here?' Milan is trying to picture the scene. He is grateful he was not there.

'She did look surprised. She left keys for you, there on the table.' Milan picks up his spare set of keys for the flat.

'That would seem to be that then.'

'It would.' Murri is looking at him carefully. She carries on cautiously.

'She was carrying a bottle of wine and a cake.'

'That sounds a bit like a peace offering to me.'

'It does, doesn't it?'

Does Milan detect a hint of triumph in Murri's attitude? Or is it his own conscience over Karen. The two of them, Karen and Murri, are strangely alike in some ways and in others very different. Both funny, tidy, drink a lot, attractive. On the other hand there is a certain recklessness in Murri compared to Karen's cautiousness.

They sit down for a late lunch.

'All morning during my teaching I've been getting nothing but *Murri, Murri, Murri* tapped out from Roma.'

'That's nice.'

'I don't understand though, how has she got the idea of

you so quickly. I wasn't even sure if she really understood who I was, never mind you.'

Murri shakes her head.

'You've got to be careful. Things aren't always what they seem. With this flood of information technique you have to be prepared for mistakes happening, misunderstandings.'

'So what do you think Roma means by *Murri*?'

Murri shrugs.

'Who knows? Who knows? Could be anything. Perhaps *Murri* to her means a certain facility with the tapping?' she says cheekily.

'Isn't that confusion a huge problem?'

'It's just part of the learning process. You make mistakes; they gradually get corrected or refined. In some ways it may not even be a mistake. If Roma is thinking the word *Murri* means a certain improved way of tapping then that is right in a way, that is part of me, just as you might think the word *Murri* has something to do with black hair or with a scooter.'

'Or with the Saturday Lunchtime Lecture Series?'

Murri narrows her eyes and blows menacingly through her pursed lips.

'Someone phoned,' she adds. 'Your cousin, I think she was called Ella. I said you'd call her back?'

'It's been like Victoria Station here this morning.'

After lunch Milan rings Ella. Predictably she immediately asks, 'Who was that who answered the phone?'

'Her name is Murri, if you must know.'

'So you have replaced Karen, was that her name? That was fast. I had you down for the caring sensitive type. Well you live and learn. She sounds young; how old is she?'

'Early twenties,' Milan answers with a sigh. He knows what's coming.

'You are turning into a bit of a cradle-snatcher, aren't you?'

'It feels more like she snatched me, whatever that's called.'

'Zimmer-snatcher, you mean?'

Milan thinks his cousin takes no prisoners.

'That's a bit unkind. I'm not that old.'

'Well when you say *cradle-snatcher* it doesn't normally mean you are going out with a one-year-old, so we can have a little leeway with Zimmer, can't we?'

Never argue with your cousin when she becomes pedantic, Milan thinks.

'If you say so.'

Later that afternoon Milan goes round to Andreas's place for emergency counselling. Andreas gets Milan a beer from the fridge.

Milan tells him the whole story of Roma, Karen and Murri. It reminds Andreas of a film he saw called Bob and two girls' names he can't remember.

'This isn't a film; this is real. I came here for words of wisdom, not Film Review.'

'Well,' Andreas tells Milan pensively, 'In that case, I must say that I can't recommend starting up a new relationship on the rebound from another.'

'Rebound? Rebound? This isn't on the rebound, I hadn't even hit the floor never mind started bounding up again.'

'Now the pre-rebound, or the pre-bound as it's known technically, that's another matter.' Andreas still does not seem to be taking this too seriously. 'What you're doing, it sounds a bit like chain-smoking, only with women, not very respectful, if you ask me.'

Milan ignores this last remark.

'I'm worried about Karen.'

'Karen is old enough and ugly enough to look after herself,' Andreas says with a hint of irony.

What Milan is really worried about is himself. How can he just let Karen walk away like that and feel almost nothing? Whatever it is that's happening to him Milan doesn't like it. If he's honest, Milan doesn't like himself at the moment.

Meanwhile Andreas is babbling on.

'Maybe if Roma hadn't turned up you two – you and Karen that is – could have been OK, but Roma isn't going to go away. It's a matter of divided attention. Murri seems to be able to cope with that.'

'I'm wondering if Murri is keener in a way on Roma than on me?'

Milan feels Roma tapping.

< More beer >

'You don't have another beer do you, Andreas?' Milan asks, 'You know I'm drinking for two here.'

As Andreas is going to the fridge he throws in a caustic, 'Your sister, you know, she never buys a round, does she?'

Two beers later and Milan is turning philosophical.

'All this business with Roma has really sensitised me to what a completely weird place we are in.'

'What, my house?' Andreas jokes. Milan pays no attention to him and carries on with his thread.

'You know, the world.'

'Oh, that old place.'

Milan can see it is going to be one of those conversations but he perseveres.

'We get so used to it that we just take it completely for granted. It's only when you have to explain it to someone who has never experienced it that you really see the strangeness of it all.'

'For example?'

'Say take drinking a glass of beer. You're holding something that is solid, and it has something liquid in it... just the difference between those two states, how strange is that? Holding it, what is that? And then you open a hole in your head, whatever head might be, and you pour the liquid in; why does it go in? What does it feel like in your mouth?'

Andreas holds up his hands.

'Hold on man, you blowin' my mind wit' your scary psychedelic trip thoughts.'

He is obviously imitating somebody from a film but the reference is lost on Milan. For the umpteenth time Milan just ignores him and carries on.

'You know what I mean?'

'Now that you mention it, it is strange, but we can't go around all the time going *this is solid, wow, this is round, amazing,* can we?'

'Why not?'

'For a start, we would sound like a bunch of drunken nineteen-year-old students talking at two in the morning about the meaning of everything, wouldn't we?'

'That,' Milan admits, 'is a fair comment.'

On his way back home, passing all the Christmas stuff in the shops, Milan starts thinking about Karen again.

He feels more tapping.

< Murri, Murri, Roma talk Murri >

Well at least someone is happy with the way things have turned out.

7

ON the first of April Murri turns up at Milan's at around half nine in the morning. Milan wonders if she is up to an April Fool's thing but no, she is very excited about a new idea.

The last four months have gone really fast. The orchestra is recording a double CD of Christmas music for next Christmas, which bled into the real Christmas concerts; it feels as if Milan has had six months of Christmas. Murri disappeared to America for the whole of February, something to do with her studies, and came back with a completely shaved head. She tried cross-Atlantic communication with Roma, but not very successfully, leaving the two of them, Milan and Roma, slightly stalled in their progress. Since her return however Roma's language is leaping and bounding. Milan is still not exactly sure what their relationship is, Murri's and his. They seem to have just stepped into something without talking about it or anything. She stays round at his place most of the time. The woman she shares her flat with,

Hannah, is not very keen on visitors. Milan has only been there twice, fairly briefly.

Murri has recently been trying to get Roma to start associating spoken words with the tapped out texts. Sometimes she tries to lecture Milan about how useful this is, seeming to forget that it was his idea in the first instance to talk to Roma normally. Now that it is working so well with the tapping Milan has not been so sure of adding further complexities. Murri can be very insistent however.

'She isn't deaf you know. In all probability her hearing is good. Now that she has a good understanding of how language works and how she can communicate, it will open up the possibility of listening to people who don't know your codes.'

Anyway, this sunny April morning there is no stopping her. She has discovered someone called Frank who works on hearing aids and implants and such things. He is very interested in helping Roma communicate. He lives just beyond Croydon and Murri offers to take Milan there on her scooter. Milan politely declines that particular offer so they jump on the train at Victoria and head down.

Frank picks them up at the station in a jeep and takes them to a battered old house.

At the back he has a laboratory full of speakers and microphones and wires. Even Milan is impressed by the level of chaos Frank has managed to create.

Forewarned of their arrival he has been doing a few experiments. He is a big man with a beard and sounds Canadian.

Frank gives them tea and then shows them a few bits and pieces.

'What I am thinking of is a kind of two-way system. First a tie clip microphone picks up your and anyone else's speech, it gets fed down through a processor to adjust the frequencies and amplify them and is then passed on to a transducer.'

Milan is learning a lot of new stuff these days.

'Transducer?'

'It's a kind of speaker that will fit on a belt around your waist in contact with your hipbone. That means it will vibrate the bone more than produce sounds like a normal speaker.'

He hands Milan the metal object. It is surprisingly heavy for its size.

'And what do you mean adjust the frequencies?'

'So, Roma is it?'

Milan nods.

'Roma's ears are embedded in pounds of flesh and bone, your flesh and bone in fact. If we can work out how that is affecting what she hears I can boost those frequencies that are being reduced so she hears more like what we do.'

'That makes sense. How do you work out the frequencies that are being cut out?'

'We shove this microphone up your ass. No only joking, I have some fresh meat and bone from the butchers here, already done a couple of experiments. Let me just measure you up.'

He puts a tape measure around Milan's waist.

'Mostly fat.'

'Is that good?'

'Not for your long term health it isn't.'

He gets out a belt thing with leads to a small box with dials on it and attaches the tiny microphone and the transducer.

As he is being strapped up Milan asks, 'This is going to affect how music sounds to her isn't it?'

Frank nods enthusiastically.

'Most definitely. In theory it should sound better. It will basically sound more like what we are hearing rather than the underwater kind of effect that she is getting at the minute. Of course we don't know how her hearing and brain processes have adapted to her conditions. On balance I think she will like it; you can always switch it off if she doesn't, can't you?'

There is no arguing with that.

'Let me just tell her what we are doing.'

Milan taps:

< Roma, new sound louder >

Milan catches Murri's eye. She is shaking her head, sadly. She always wants him to move away from his baby talk as she calls it to more normal speech. It is Milan who is the baby though in terms of the tapping. He simply can't do it fast enough to make whole long sentences with prepositions and whatever – by the time Milan gets to tapping in the end of a long sentence he can't remember how it started.

< Roma ready > Roma nearly always talks to Milan in kind. Isn't she being a little patronising he sometimes wonders?

Milan puts on the belt. Frank adjusts it and the tiny tie clip mike. He switches on. A terrible feedback noise blares out. He quickly turns it down.

< Ouch > comes from Roma.

Milan taps back < Sorry. Try again >

This time all Milan can feel is a slight echoey buzz around his waist.

We need to try a bit of music, Milan thinks.

'Do you have a radio or something?'

Frank fetches out a battered old ghetto blaster with a radio in it. Milan quickly finds Classic FM. It is playing Vivaldi's *Four Seasons*, surprise surprise. Milan puts it at normal listening volume to his ears.

< OK, Roma, louder? >

< Louder >

Frank adjusts the pickup box. Milan realises that he is not going to have to listen to music at home at hyper volumes any more.

Eventually they have an < OK > on loudness.

< Listen Roma, better or worse? >

Frank adjusts the frequencies.

Milan responds with thumbs up and down until the adjustments have reached optimal listening quality for Roma.

'Now for the other way.' Frank brings out another belt.

'I am going to be strapped up like a monkey,' Milan protests.

Frank nods.

'These are just prototypes at the minute. I'll get them all on one belt for you eventually and not so bulky.'

This belt contains a pick-up, which goes on the other side of the hip bone and connects up to a speaker box. Frank turns up the volume and the sound of Roma's tapping fills the room.

'She can shout now,' says Murri excitedly. She claps a message near Milan's microphone.

Back comes Roma:

< Not so loud, Murri >

Frank has even got wires that will connect the belts to a mobile phone if they want.

'That's not much use to me,' Milan jokes.

He can already see it. Murri abroad ringing Roma up for a half-hour conversation.

Murri is also thinking ahead.

'It's a shame your code is so idiosyncratic. Still I am sure there would be plenty of people willing to put the effort into learning it to speak to her. The more conversation she gets the better for her language skills.'

'It's only Morse code, sort of,' Milan defends himself. 'We, that is Roma and me, have made a couple of improvements; some of the letters were hard to emphasise at speed.'

On the train back to Victoria Murri encourages Milan to speak every word he taps in to Roma for when they get the new devices.

Milan thinks to himself that he is going to look like the village idiot walking down Oxford Street talking away to himself, to his imaginary friend, even.

A week later a parcel arrives in the post. Milan was expecting one belt, but it contains two. Murri grabs one of them.

'This one's for me.'

Milan raises his eyes questioningly.

'I asked Frank to do a short-range radio version. Look it has a tapping patch on it the same as yours and another speaker. When I am in the same room as you I can talk to Roma too.'

'Well I suppose it is a bit more sightly than having you stuffing your hands down my pants in public,' Milan agrees. They put them on. They are very neat. Murri finds the radio tapping less sensitive than the more direct approach. Milan is secretly pleased with the thought that it might slow her down a bit. Milan puts his thimbles away in a drawer.

They go to Andreas's private view that evening to test-drive the new toys. Murri is wearing a sari instead of her usual punkish outfit. If anything this makes her look stranger with her piercings and shaved head. The exhibition is in a nice white gallery in Cork Street. They have to get there early as ordered, so that it doesn't look empty when the real people arrive.

Andreas is psyching himself up to do a big sell. His two daughters are there standing with his ex-wife whose name Milan can never remember. Her name is in there somewhere, round a corner of his brain, but which corner he doesn't know.

They start the preview tour. Andreas is very proud.

'Now Roma is one person that I would like to impress but who will never know what a great artist I am.'

Milan leans forward pretending he is going to touch the surface of one of the pictures.

'I could tell her how good they are for you?'

Andreas gently grabs his arm.

'It's not the same; that would just be word of mouth. You would say how great I was, wouldn't you? How could she tell if you were lying or not? In fact she doesn't even know where she is. For all she knows everything you tell her could just be made up.'

They move on to a large red and green canvas. Andreas continues, 'I've got an idea to tackle the 'where she is' thing. By the way this one isn't dry yet.'

Milan pretends to wipe his fingers on his jacket.

'What is your idea then?' Murri asks.

'Use musical metaphors to tell her her location – *inside, outside, next to...*'

Andreas puts his arms out and does a *ta-ta* sound.

It actually sounds like a good idea for once but Milan doesn't give him the satisfaction.

'Might work,' Milan answers grudgingly.

Murri taps to him:

< It sounds like a good idea >

Milan taps back:

< I know, but don't tell him >

In an instant they have unthinkingly discovered a secret means of communication. Every couple should have one, Milan thinks. Maybe they could patent it.

Roma butts in:

< What idea? >

< Tell you later > taps back Murri.

Milan feels like one of the three musketeers.

< All for one > Milan taps.

< And one for all > comes back from Murri.

< Beer? > suggests Roma. Milan manages to get a glass of terrible French wine from a box. He forces it down for

Roma's sake. In her eyes all wines are equal. Milan mentions the wine to Andreas.

'If your gallery shelled out a few quid on decent wine then people might actually drink enough to buy your paintings.'

'Thanks,' replies the artist, 'but if you think anyone who is going to buy one of my paintings would drink this stuff you are sadly mistaken. This is purely for the hangers-on, like you, to build up a bit of crowd.'

'Even hangers-on have standards,' Milan replies defensively.

Murri jumps in just then using the belt to reach new heights or is that depths of hypocrisy, 'These paintings are gorgeous,' she tells a beaming Andreas to his face while tapping a big < NOT > to Milan.

She has a certain streak of cruelty in her Milan thinks.

Andreas's youngest daughter, Lisa, starts hanging around with them. She hears Murri say that they are losing an hour this evening by moving to summer-time.

'Where do all the hours go?' she asks.

Andreas adjusts his glasses and looks upwards poetically.

'They are stored at Parliament House, one for each person,' he informs his daughter.

'Doesn't that take up a lot of space?'

These two seem a bit like Morecambe and Wise to Milan. He's starting to wonder if they have rehearsed all this.

'You know it would if they were all at their original size. A normal hour is about as big as a pumpkin but they can be compressed down to the size of a match head as they are mostly made of air.'

'What happens to them then?'

'Well they pump them back up and return them to everyone in the autumn, of course. You've heard of inflation haven't you?'

Lisa nods, not looking entirely convinced.

'What if someone dies, in between?'

'In that case their spare hours are given to the new-born babies.'

'What if someone gets back someone else's hour, the wrong one?'

'If it is a hard working person's hour then good luck to them. If they get a lazy hour well that's just tough.'

'I want to keep my own hour this year.'

'Well you better go and write a letter to Parliament about it, hadn't you?'

She scurries off to try and find a piece of paper to write her letter.

'Why do you tell her all this bollocks?' Milan intervenes.

'It's good for the imagination,' is all Andreas can muster, though he is not clear whose imagination they are talking about.

Murri taps to Milan:

< What an arsehole >

Milan taps a reply:

< He may be an arsehole, but he's my arsehole >

Murri starts laughing.

Milan says out loud, 'I didn't mean it exactly like that.'

Andreas and Roma appear to be equally confused.

Later back at Milan's place they start on Andreas's idea about the word *inside*. Milan gets out his Casio electronic keyboard. He plays a C and a G together.

And then Murri taps the word < Inside > and Milan plays the E in the middle.

They get an < E > tapped back with Roma's perfect pitch.

Murri taps:

< Yes E yes inside >

Milan then plays the two notes again this time putting the E above the pair.

Murri taps:

< No inside, yes outside >

No response.

Then Milan does the same thing with half a dozen other chords to get away from any association with the actual notes themselves.

Now that the tutorial is over they test Roma out. She is one hundred percent accurate with notes being inside and outside of the others.

And so they go for the big one.

Murri taps:

< Roma inside Milan. Milan outside Roma >

There is a long silence, maybe half an hour.

Then they hear < Roma inside Milan, Roma inside Milan > maybe fifty times.

To celebrate their achievement Murri takes off her sari under which she has been wearing nothing but the belt.

Two minutes later lying on the floor, Murri, on top as usual, taps on Milan's forehead:

< Milan inside Murri, Milan inside Murri >

They both laugh.

Thank God, Milan thinks, Murri didn't let Roma hear what she just said.

That would have taken weeks of unexplaining.

8

With the new belts Roma's speech has moved up another gear over the last month and a half. Murri has taken to speaking out loud as she taps – perhaps to keep Milan up with them as much as anything. They can both tap more than twice as quickly as he can. Milan is surprised at that, him with his musician's fingers. Maybe it's more of a mental thing than a physical one. Milan has to think in one language and then translate. It takes him time. These two seem to think in clicks.

< Good morning, Roma. The sun is shining and it is a lovely summer day, the birds are singing. Milan is just going to make me delicious coffee. Aren't you? Yes, he's opening the coffee jar, he's putting coffee in the filter. He's boiling the water. Can you hear it? Yes. Oh what a delicious smell >

Milan knows her cramming theory and all that but he is impressed with Murri's optimism over some of the words she just throws in, for example *shining, smell, filter.* Who knows?

The piece of music tentatively titled *Roma One* has also progressed substantially. Three new melodies have been added to the original, as well as harmony, a development section, a scant disregard for conventional key structures. It is too complex for Milan to manage on his Casio now that Roma has started specifying different instruments for the parts.

He plays it to Murri on his keyboard anyway.

'What sound is that meant to be?' she asks screwing up her face.

'It's a trumpet of course.'

'Oh silly of me.'

Actually all the different instruments on the keyboard sound pretty much the same when you put them together.

In a way Milan quite likes the fact that the sounds are so artificial. When you hear a real trumpet or whatever afterwards you really appreciate it afresh in a way that you never would if you had only ever heard the real thing – a bit like how you appreciate real orange juice much more if all you have been drinking is the reconstituted stuff.

The Casio will not do for Roma however.

Milan has therefore laboriously copied the parts out and presented them to the orchestra. He is dubious about the instrumentation. A few of the instruments seem to be playing out of their ranges.

The orchestra schedule to squeeze it in in the middle of a Haydn rehearsal. At the end of the run-through there is a stunned silence, then a clattering of bows on music stands and warm applause. Milan gets up and does a mock bow pointing at his middle.

'Not the world's greatest piece of music,' Milan says to Daphne as he sits down, wondering at the same time whether he has a parental sense of pride over Roma and is fishing for a compliment.

Daphne however does not oblige and says, rather unkindly in his opinion, 'Well, as Dr Johnston said of the dog who walks on two legs: it is a wonder that he does it at all. It is after all her first piece.'

'I thought it was quite good really,' Milan answers her grumpily.

'What are you doing for your party piece?' Daphne changes the subject.

Every year George has a big orchestra party at his mansion. He made a lot of money in his youth playing sessions for pop bands. This year Roma and Milan are going to perform Steve Reich's *Clapping Music*. Usually two people perform it by clapping their hands in these patterns. They start with the same rhythm repeated twelve times; then one of the two shifts it by one note out of step with the other and so on until the whole pattern comes back full circle. It's a very exciting piece. Roma has been taking on the harder shifting pattern while Milan just taps the one that stays the same. Frank has made them a lead that can connect to a stereo system and Milan wires them up to George's on the night, nice and loud. Milan is a bit nervous, or is it Roma who is nervous? Milan has told her a lot of people will be listening but who knows what she makes of that? Anyhow they perform it faultlessly. This time the rest of the orchestra go wild with cheering, whistling and stamping and Milan and Roma have to repeat the whole thing. George even suggests that they should record it and send it to the composer retitled *Tapping Music*.

Roma's picture is on the cover of *Life Magazine*. She is getting quite famous these days. Milan asked them not to include his picture in the article. Not that it makes much difference with the occasional photographer still hanging around. The media seems to vacillate between thinking Milan is a big hoaxer on the one hand and on the other that there may be a real story there – but not a very interesting one, one of the rewards for leading a boring life Milan supposes. He does get recognised quite a lot however; in fact a kid even stood up for him on the bus to give him his seat, his friends pissing themselves laughing. The *Life Magazine* picture of Roma however is one of the nicer ones. The scans are just information on surfaces and shapes, although the computer can colour them in how you like. But but this version is a bit like a line drawing and Roma looks a little like a seahorse. Milan puts it with his copies of *Nature* and *Scientific American* that also feature Roma on the cover.

Like both those other magazines the *Life* article concentrates on the physical qualities of Roma's form and the general principle of conjoined twins. They all skate lightly over the, to them, unresolved question of whether she is alive or not. After all Milan has refused numerous offers of tests which would prove that she were. Milan shows Andreas one of the letters from a big American university offering him a hundred thousand dollars for two months of tests.

'Why not do it?' Andreas asks.

'At the minute we are just a curiosity. If everyone was convinced Roma was alive – and communicating – the publicity floodgates would open. Besides I don't really need the money and the orchestra just doesn't sound the same without me.'

Two lies in one sentence, not bad.

On the May bank holiday Murri and Roma and Milan go down to Oxford for the day. The train is packed. Murri is as ever clicking all the way, though Milan has asked her to stop speaking out loud in public. Near Reading Milan recognises long familiar rotes in the patterns they are making. It is the seven times table.

'We started on them a couple of days ago,' Murri explains. 'Roma wanted to surprise you.'

Even more people get on at the station. It seems as if the whole world is heading for Oxford.

'Well I am surprised,' Milan answers, 'Mainly by why you are teaching her all that stuff. I mean, what use is arithmetic to her?'

Murri is shaking her head sadly at him.

'You still don't get it do you? You think too practically. What Roma needs are structures, different ways of thinking, probably even more than we do because she has comparatively so little to go on. Besides, the practical uses will become apparent in time. She needs numbers for composing for example, then there is time itself, then geography and history, distance...'

'Alcohol content could be useful,' Milan acquiesces and decides to stay quiet in future. Luckily they pull in to Oxford just then. Milan is starting to see the tenacity and drive of Murri the teacher. No wonder her pupils do so well with her behind them.

In Oxford Murri has a short meeting with someone at one of the colleges and then they decide to go on a boat on the river. They choose one of the small ones that you paddle with your feet. By ducking under some wires they manage to lose the bank holiday crowds. They both hear the tapping < Orgasm soon? >

Murri rocks the boat from side to side to tease Roma. She even taps in a few:

< Oh, oh, ohs >

Milan thinks Murri can be cruel at times.

'We will never know what is going through her head,' Milan says to Murri ruefully.

Murri however sees another learning opportunity and launches into the task of describing the difference between liquids and solids.

'Don't forget gases too,' Milan mentions helpfully.

How strange it is that where Milan sees difficulties Murri sees opportunities.

9

MURRI is shaking her head in disbelief. They are having a lazy Sunday morning in bed. Milan has been reading the papers. Murri and Roma have been rabbiting on.

'What is it now?' Milan asks, holding his breath.

'She's taking the mickey out of you.'

'Who is? Roma?'

'Yes, little Roma is making a monkey out of her big brother.'

'How is she doing it?'

'She's imitating you, imitating your tapping voice.'

'Tapping voice?' Now Milan is shaking his head in wonder.

'Yes, everyone knows that each person's tapping is as individual as their spoken voice. Yours in fact is particularly distinctive.'

Everyone knows? This is news to Milan.

'In what way?'

'Well, for a start you go at about two miles an hour.

Honestly someone could die waiting for you to finish a sentence.'

'And?'

'And then there are your *b*-s. They have a kind of stutter in the middle and you muddle up your *f*-s and *l*-s...'

'Are you saying that I have a kind of tapping impediment?' Milan is vaguely hurt.

'Not me, mister, it's your sister who's making the jokes.'

Milan decides to take the bull by the horns,

< Roma, I am deeply saddened by your behaviour >

Milan is not even that sure she knows what *behaviour* means. He gets back:

< Deeply, deeply sorry for any offence >

Murri is pissing herself laughing and Milan has a strange internal feeling, a feeling that his sister might be laughing too.

Later that morning the girls have another surprise for him. Murri draws out a noughts and crosses board on a piece of paper. She taps < Ready > to Roma who answers:

< Milan to go first >

Murri hands him the pencil and nods.

Milan puts down a cross. Murri has numbered each of the squares for his benefit.

< Two > Milan taps in.

< Five > comes back. Murri indicates the middle square rather patronisingly. Milan puts in a circle there.

They draw the first game.

The next one Roma starts, once again a five. Milan carelessly, or maybe not so carelessly, enters a four. Murri raises her eyebrows questioningly but Roma is already tapping < One, one, one >

Milan obediently puts her nought in the first square and is of course soundly thrashed.

They play maybe ten times, the best Milan can do is a draw.

'Don't worry,' says Murri consolingly, 'I can't beat her either.'

'Giving her more structures?' Milan asks Murri.

'Spatial concepts, abstraction, competition, identity, all that kind of stuff. But also it's fun; she likes playing.'

'So what's next then, chess?'

'That's possible. I was also thinking of *Go*.' She laughs.

Lisa, Andreas's youngest daughter, the one with the hour concerns, wants to come round and see them, Milan, Murri and Roma. She wants to bring a friend.

The two of them arrive rather sheepishly. Milan asks the other girl what her name is. The two crease up laughing. What is it with me? Milan thinks. He seems to be the cause of universal merriment these days. Eventually Lisa manages to splutter through her laughter.

'Her – name – is – Roma!'

Milan decides that formal introductions might calm things down.

< Roma, meet another Roma >

In actual fact Roma has so far not come across two people with the same name, even the composers that she knows of. Milan sees that Murri is itching to seize another learning opportunity but he decides to clarify matters to Roma himself.

< You are Roma Kotzia and this other girl is Roma – >

Milan is speaking as he taps. The girl tells him her surname is Morpeth.

< This is Roma Morpeth >

'Are you called Roma after the city in Italy?' Milan asks her.

Lisa butts in with, 'No, she's called after the woman who is in the TV programme where she is an angel.'

'And she comes and makes everything better and then at the end she just disappears.'

'And they turn around and say *Where is she? I never said thank you to her.*'

'We watch it on Sunday mornings.'

At last Milan manages to get a word in between them, 'Sounds good, someone to sort things out, I should watch it.'

'It's not on at the minute,' Lisa informs him patiently.

'Maybe you could let me know when it starts again?'

Lisa nods.

'Roma has a question.' She nudges her friend.

Once again they dissolve into fits of giggles.

Eventually Roma Two recovers enough breath to ask,

'Is she naked?'

'Is she stark naked?' clarifies Lisa.

The new Roma doesn't seem to like her question being hijacked like this.

'What is stark naked, then?' she asks.

Lisa thinks, then, 'It's even more naked than naked. It's extra specially naked.'

Milan looks at Murri and raises his eyes. The tiny debate carries on.

'How can you be more naked than naked?' Roma Two demands.

This is like a meeting of the Little Miss Linguist Club, Milan thinks.

'You can!' Lisa shouts.

They both look at him for his judgement.

Milan passes the buck to Murri who as ever has an answer.

'*Stark naked* means you are naked but really exposed. You could be naked but hiding behind a bush. That would be just *naked*. But if you were standing naked on top of a hill. That could be *stark naked*.'

Both girls seem to take this as confirmation of their own point of view.

Lisa returns to the point.

'But is Roma stark naked?'

'Which Roma?' Milan answers provoking another collapse into giggles.

Eventually Roma Two recovers enough to confirm, 'Not me! Your Roma.'

'Well, she is definitely not stark naked. In a way you could say she is naked but I am her clothes. I provide the warmth and also cover her modesty.'

Murri has been communicating all this stuff to Roma. Roma herself is highly interested in just what these clothes things that they are talking about are. The two of them enter into a tirade of questions and explanations involving fabric, nudity and babies. Meanwhile Milan gets the girls glasses of orange juice. They are fascinated by the speed of Murri's tapping and the last Milan sees of them they are going down the street, tapping endlessly on each other's arms.

That evening Murri and Milan go out for dinner to a vegetarian restaurant. Murri seems preoccupied with something, nervous almost. She is describing the place to Roma. Milan can just about follow because he can look around. If Milan was relying only on the tapping he would be lost, but Roma seems to be keeping up. Murri tells her firmly that it is a non-smoking restaurant. Roma suggests they go somewhere else. They overrule her.

The food is very good and Milan has a sickly desert for Roma to make up for her nicotine deprivation. All through the meal Murri's agitation has not decreased. If anything it is greater.

Finally she bursts out, 'You need to see this.'

She pulls a folded magazine out of her bag. She is looking worried, very worried in fact.

Milan takes the magazine. It's an American medical journal he has never seen before with very dense type and no pictures. It is opened at an article entitled *Communicating with an Isolate,* and its author is Murriam Khambaty. Milan stops reading.

'What?' Milan looks at her.

'It's part of my PhD thesis. My supervisor advised me to publish it early.'

'You're doing a PhD? You're doing a PhD thesis on Roma?' Without realising it Milan has half stood up.

Murri stares straight into his eyes, unflinching.

'It isn't entirely about Roma; it's about special communication techniques, but the developments with Roma have become a central theme of my work now. It's original research, unique. It's groundbreaking.'

Milan slowly sits down again in his chair.

'It's heartbreaking, more like.'

Milan reads out aloud the abstract at the top of the article.

'The subject of the study is a multi-sensory deprived (visual, touch, taste) forty-two-year-old.'

Milan looks back at her, '*The subject of the study?*'

'Those are just normal terms, it's a dispassionate scientific article, you can't write my dear friend Roma who...'

'*Dear friend?* Some dear friend,' Milan cuts her off.

He forces himself to read more of the article. It catalogues words, techniques, small progresses. There are a lot of references to other books and articles, arguments. Even through the cloud of his anger Milan is secretly impressed. He had always thought Murri was smart but this stuff is in another league.

'You've done all this in secret?'

'I knew it would be difficult for you.'

Milan is suddenly conscious that all this time Murri has been tapping to Roma. Milan is too distracted to follow completely but he gets the idea that Roma has known something of this and has been warned it might be difficult. Milan switches off the receiver on his belt. It seems like a very aggressive act, like snatching the telephone out of their hands.

'You're only with us, with me, so you can study Roma. This whole thing has just been a research project for you.'

'No! I love Roma as much as you do.'

'I need time to think about this. I think I should go.' Milan stands up again and makes for the door. Murri sits in her seat.

'Let me say goodbye,' she nods at Roma.

'No.' Milan is beside himself with anger now.

As Milan is leaving Murri quickly claps:

< Goodbye Roma, love you >

Milan can feel the tiny response in him:

< Murri Murri speak to me >

Milan is not sure if it is from Roma or from himself.

Outside Milan realises he still has the journal in his hand.

Back at his flat he sits for a while in the dark. For a time Milan feels utterly alone and then he remembers his sitting tenant. He will never be by himself again.

What was that old cigarette advert? *You're never alone with a Strand* or something and a film of a guy in a hat on a street corner slowly killing himself with a cigarette. Wonder if they sold a lot.

Milan tries to speak to Roma but she has gone into a sulk. He thinks she picked up quite a lot of what happened in the restaurant. He resorts to emergency measures.

< Whisky for Roma? >

Milan feels like a mum with a difficult child bribing it with a lollipop. But he needs to talk.

She leaves a pause just to let him know how upset she is and then answers:

< OK, a big one >

Milan pours them both a big one. Cheap round Milan thinks. Always two drinks for the price of one with us.

He decides to put on some pop music. It seems more apt than a classical piece in this case. Milan lets her choose.

< What song do you want? Not classical, OK? >

< *Passenger* > she says appropriately enough. Milan finds his *Greatest Punk Songs Ever* CD and puts it in the player.

< Do you like the words or the music? > Milan asks her.

< The music. Can't understand the words. Too fast >
she replies.

Milan plays the track.

< These words you should know >

Milan taps the words to Roma as it plays:

< I am a passenger

And I ride and I ride

I ride through the city's backside

I see the stars come out of the sky

Yeah, they're bright in a hollow sky

You know it looks so good tonight >

By the time they get to the end of the second verse
the whisky is kicking in and Roma is joining in on the
refrain:

< Singin' la la, la la, la-la-la la

La la, la la, la-la-la la

La la, la la, la-la-la la, la-la >

10

MILAN gets a message from Professor Conway on his answer machine. Guiltily he realises that he has never reported back to her over the last nine months.

He rings her.

'This is very delicate; it's about Murri,' she says.

'Murri, you know her then?' Milan is surprised. His mind is racing back to the end of last year. Conway sent him to the teaching centre but not directly to Murri. But then she would probably know Milan would end up with her anyway.

'I'm her PhD supervisor.'

For the second time in his life Milan nearly puts the phone down on Conway.

This Milan wants to hear, however.

'You set me up with her?' Milan is speaking very carefully.

'In a manner of speaking. I knew it would be useful for both parties; she was easily the best person to help you, and at the same time I knew it would give her a push with her studies.

The romantic side of things I never envisaged. I suspected it might be problematic when Murri told me that...'

Milan cuts her off, 'Your point in phoning is?'

'Yes, well, Murri is a very brilliant researcher. Her work will have enormous benefits to future generations. I would like you to reconsider allowing her access to Roma, for Roma's benefit as much as hers.'

'She asked you to call me?'

'Not at all. Murri is firmly of the belief that you will not speak to her ever again or allow Roma to. I am asking you personally.'

'The answer is no. Murri was right about that. Not now or ever,' Milan answers.

There is a short pause on the phone. And then, 'Have you asked your sister about that? I'm not sure if it is fair for you to make this kind of decision for her. She has some rights too you know.'

This takes him back a bit. On the one hand it seems like a kind of underhand manipulative trick, but on the other there is a grain of truth in it. What right does Milan have to decide who Roma talks to?

He makes up his mind to focus on the underhand trick possibility rather than the grain of truth one. Of course Roma has rights, but the situation is that they have to live with each other, and an element of compromise is necessary. And anyway, who are these two to lecture him on morality?

'I have discussed it with Roma and she agrees with me that it is best if we don't have any more contact with Murri,' Milan lies.

Milan feels the professor and Murri will both know this is not true, but what can they say?

'If that really is the case then I am simply very sorry that it has ended up this way.'

'You and me both.'

Milan puts the phone down.

Andreas's daughter, Lisa, is staying with him for the weekend, instead of with his ex-wife as normal. Milan is summoned as guest of honour, although he suspects more as an entertainment or maybe even a diversion.

'No, no,' Andreas assures Milan, 'this is a personal request from Lisa herself. She wants to ask you more questions; she is even tempted to try to speak to Roma herself.'

Milan agrees to go – maybe it will stop him thinking about the Murri business.

Lisa has an amazing amount of clothes on: jumpers, tights, skirts, at least three of each. She is much calmer without her friend.

'Where is Murri?' she asks immediately.

'She's busy,' Milan avoids the question with an answer that is not really a lie after all.

"How old are you?' Milan asks her.

'Six.'

'That's a good age.'

'What's a bad age?' she replies tartly.

Milan thinks he had better watch what he says here.

'Well, one year old for a start when you're pooping all over the place.' This answer seems to satisfy her.

'Your dad said you have a few questions for Roma?'

'Yes, I do.'

'Go on then.'

Lisa thinks for a while.

'Hmmm, is she, I mean Roma, ever afraid?'

That surprises him. *Out of the mouths of babes* and all that. Milan stalls for time, 'Afraid of what?'

'Afraid of the dark maybe?'

'I don't know if you can be afraid of the dark if you only know the dark.'

She does not pursue the afraid question. Maybe Milan will return to it later himself.

'Is she thirsty?'

'Yes she gets thirsty, definitely.'

'But she can't drink anything.'

'No, but I can. She tells me if she is thirsty, although I'm usually already thirsty myself and then I have something to drink and so she isn't thirsty anymore.'

'But if her mouth gets dry?'

'We don't even know if she has a mouth.'

This has taken her aback a little, touché.

'Can I speak to her?'

'Yes, you tell me something to say and I will tap it in to her, and you can hear if she taps back and I'll tell you what it means.' Milan turns up the amplifier on his belt so that she can hear clearly.

'Hello. I am Lisa.'

'OK.'

Milan does his stuff.

'She says, 'hello. I am Roma.'

'I like Abba.'

'I like Abba too.'

'My eyes are blue.'

'Sorry, we don't do eyes and we don't know colours.' This is not strictly true. Murri in her cramming phase was always talking about eyes and colours including blue, especially blue as it had been on his list of impossible words, the ones that she had scored out. When was that? Six months ago? Roma herself talks about them too, colours and eyes, but it is one of those grey areas where Milan is not convinced she actually knows what she is talking about. In this instance Milan thinks it wisest to stick to safe subjects.

Lisa is not to be diverted and startles him with her next question.

'Is she blind then?'

'We don't really know for sure, but it's dark in there, remember, and there is not a lot to see.'

She gives this answer some thought. And then, 'Shouldn't they make a little hole in you for her to look out of then?'

It is such an obvious idea. Milan is struck by the fact that no one has come up with it so far.

'That's a very interesting thought. Maybe I could ask the doctors what they think about it.'

'She could have one of those things that we have on our door where you look out through, a kind of spyglass thing.'

'I know what you mean.'

'What if she needs the toilet?'

'I do that for her.'

'And does she cry?'

'I think she feels sad.'

'That's all for now.'

'Now? You mean there's going to be more?'

'Yes, I have to cogitate first.'

'Cogitate?'

'It means to think.'

'Yes, I thought so. You know a lot of good words.'

'You'd be surprised.'

As she is leaving the room, a parting shot, 'You should read her stories.'

'Good idea.'

'Tell her bye.'

Milan does.

'She says bye back.'

11

For several days after the meeting with Lisa, Milan can't get the idea out of his head of letting Roma see out through a hole in his side. It's so simple and obvious a concept.

Eventually Milan rings Lister. After all these months and considering how angry he had been during their last conversation Milan feels a bit sheepish but Lister is surprisingly friendly. He asks him to come in and see him.

Two days later in Lister's office Milan explains the concept and Lister immediately picks it up and runs with it.

'It wouldn't be a technically difficult operation but you want someone who has a lot of abdominal experience. I have a colleague; we were at medical school together, his name is Strangelove.'

'Is he a doctor?' Milan has to ask.

Lister puts his hands up, palms forward, 'Don't even think about it. He has had it for twenty years; he has heard everything, just put his name out of your mind.'

'He could change it by deed poll or something?'

'He doesn't want to. He is proud of it. He is toughing it out.'

In the pub with Andreas, Milan mentions his new doctor's famous name. Andreas goes off into one of his routines. After a few barely passable Peter Sellers impressions he goes on to tell Milan that he has heard of a medical condition where the patient is unable to control their hand or arm which is now called *Strangelove Syndrome*. One person even had the foot version. In order to shut him up Milan cruelly asks how many pictures he has sold from his new exhibition.

Two days later the receptionist calls out Milan's name and asks him to go in and see the doctor.

Hoping to provoke her into saying his name, Milan cannot resist asking, 'Which doctor?'

She looks at him for an extra second. She is obviously used to this.

'No, he's just a regular doctor.'

'That will be the one.'

She points to one of the doors.

'Better not keep the doctor waiting?'

'Better not.'

Milan goes into Dr Strangelove's office. Milan has been in so many of these places he feels he could write a good surgery guide with stars and recommendations. Milan gives this one four syringes out of five.

Strangelove, it turns out, is maybe his favourite doctor, completely down to earth and not in the least doctorish.

Milan jumps in as usual at the deep end, 'Someone suggested to me that you could bore a peephole in my stomach so that my sister Roma can look out.'

Strangelove nods. Like Lister he is not immediately dismissive.

'That's interesting. Was it another doctor who suggested it?'

'No, it was a six-year-old girl.'

Strangelove closes his eyes. He is thinking.

'Well there are two questions. Firstly, will it work? Does Roma have the necessary visual apparatus to actually see and would she be able to make sense of what she was seeing? And secondly, what would be the physical repercussions of such a procedure not only on you but on her? Thirdly...'

'You said two questions.'

'Yes, but thirdly, what would be the benefit to her of doing all this?'

'Say you had a blind forty-two-year-old woman with cataracts you wouldn't hesitate to operate on her, would you, to let her see again?'

Strangelove nods, 'No, that's true, I wouldn't hesitate in that case, but this is different and it is still a serious question. What would be the improvement in Roma's life?

Would we be doing this just so you can teach her more easily?'

Milan has been considering this very question for several days. 'It's not just that, in fact it's everything. She could learn to read, watch TV, see Niagara Falls, see herself in fact. She has no idea of what she looks like...'

Strangelove has got the point, 'OK, OK. Let's consider the first two questions in that case. The answers to them might make the third somewhat academic after all. Let's look at the scans.'

He puts a well-worn CD into his computer and the familiar form of Roma's skeleton appears on his screen. He zooms in on the head and rotates the image around. He zooms in further. Then he superimposes another set of scans, the MRI, Milan is fairly sure. Finally he makes his pronouncement, 'The left eye does not seem to have any chance of functioning but the right eye looks promising.'

He does a few more rotations and superimposes a grid on the images.

'Her right eye is about three and a half centimetres from your skin surface, and luckily there are no bones in the way. There are all sorts of risks however, number one being infection. Let me speak to my colleagues. I know someone who deals with tracheotomies and Jameson who has done a lot of colostomies. We need a good eye specialist as well.'

'This is very kind of you.'

'No need for thanks. We'll be making history after all.'

Five days later they all meet up. The collective enthusiasm of the group of doctors is actually off-putting. Milan had been gearing up to overcome their disapproval, but this positiveness puts him off instead. Perhaps he had been hoping to be dissuaded? Does he really want a permanent hole in his stomach? They have even brought in a contraption for him to look through.

Strangelove explains, 'This is a three and a half centimetre superflexible stent, one centimetre in diameter with a fish-eye lens. We were initially thinking we would have to remove the eyelid, but Dr Scott here,' he points to the eye surgeon, 'strongly disapproves of that.'

Dr Scott sounds more Welsh than Scottish, 'You can't just let someone's eye hang around in space. You need the blinking action and tear ducts to keep the eye healthy. Everything with the patient here looks to be in place although we can't tell from the scans if the eye will properly function, in fact even when we see the eye we can't tell. It's a case of suck it and see. We're now thinking that we could have a small cavity in front of the eye. We could make skin grafts from the end of the stent to the tissue surrounding the eye. The lens at our end could be removable so the eye and the tube could be periodically cleansed with a saline solution.'

Dr Strangelove takes over, 'That should give you new words for your Roma, *liquid*, *wash*, *bath* even.'

Horrible shock more like, Milan is thinking.

Strangelove snaps his folder shut, 'There you are. Now you have the gruesome details do you still want to go down this road? We don't see any medical problems. If the worst comes to the worst we could simply remove the stent and sew you back up like you were before. The psychological impact on Roma of such a setback is more difficult to predict, but you know her better than we do.'

Scott is overwhelmingly enthusiastic by now, 'We have experience of people who have never seen before, let's say from cataracts or something and it does work. The brain can readjust and learn even at Roma's age. My initial worries about the narrow sightline and directing the line of vision don't seem so major now. I had been measuring her visual possibilities against normal sight, but compared to nothing the improvement will be enormous.'

Milan pleads for time to think it all over.

Murri has left a message on his answer machine. It is the first time Milan has heard her voice in several weeks. She is definitely not in favour of the operation – how she has heard about it is a mystery to him, through Lister, via Conway, Milan supposes. She talks a lot about the cochlear implant issue where children who are aurally impaired lose their identity and sense of community when they can hear again with their new implants. Milan never agreed with that whole argument anyway when he and Murri had discussed it in the past; if it was him who couldn't hear Milan would want the implant. The whole analogy is anyway irrelevant. Roma isn't part of a group of insiders who she would be deserting when she got her sight.

Milan also has an ill-defined feeling of personal bias on Murri's part. After all, if Roma starts seeing, everything is changed. She would no longer be the same impaired person, the same victim that she was, the same research subject – in fact she can already hear, and feel, if she could see as well…! Milan feels himself warming to the idea of the operation again.

Ten minutes later Milan presses the erase button on the answer machine with a certain determination, any doubts which the doctors gave him are now gone.

Milan decides to canvas Andreas's opinion; after all, his daughter started it all off.

Andreas, as strongly as Murri was against it, is in favour of the operation.

'You absolutely can't deny her her sight. It will open up a whole new world for her, literally.'

Here he goes again. As soon as someone is negative Milan becomes more sure it's a good thing, but when someone is enthusiastic, Milan goes off the idea.

'The whole thing still seems so freakish to me.'

Andreas makes a face, 'Freakish? You are already in that place. You are the ultimate freak.'

'I don't know. At the minute everything seems contained. I always found that the parallel with someone having a baby was helpful. People seem to be able to accept Roma with that thought in their minds. But foetuses don't peer out at the world through tiny tubes.'

Andreas is not to be dissuaded, 'Well, just remember, that argument has nothing to do with Roma but is entirely to do with you. She is not conscious of being a freak.'

On his way home Milan is kicking himself for falling yet again into the trap of only thinking of himself. Milan recalls Professor Conway's final comments about him deciding things for Roma. All this heart searching about the operation and Milan hasn't even asked Roma herself. He seems to be hiding behind the stupid idea that she doesn't know enough to make a reasonable decision.

< Roma, we can try something new? >

< New music? >

< No >

< Maybe new food? >

< No >

< New drink? >

< No >

< New drugs? >

Milan can see what's important to her, as if he didn't know.

< No. New new >

< New new? >

< You have the chance to see light. You could have vision. Eight days from now >

Milan is fairly convinced all this vision and light stuff means nothing to her at the minute, nothing yet he should say. Maybe it will change her life.

Milan taps in:

< What do you think? >

< Why not? >

< Roma says yes? > Milan reverts to baby speak for this decision. He wants it clear to both of them.

< Roma says yes > she answers.

Here we go then, Milan thinks to himself.

The great debate has arisen as to whether to go for a general or a local anaesthetic. Which will be more traumatic for her? Eventually the general is decided on with Strangelove there to communicate with Roma if she wakes up before Milan. Strangelove has already and very enthusiastically started learning the codes for useful phrases.

Half way through the meeting Scott suddenly pipes up, 'I've been doing a bit of background reading. What I have been thinking is, if Roma and Milan are conjoined twins, they would normally be identical twins wouldn't they?'

The implications don't really sink in for Milan.

'What I mean is, in that case, Roma would actually be male, wouldn't she?'

Milan can see from Strangelove and the other doctors' faces that this is something they have already thought about.

Strangelove even seems vaguely cross that Scott has brought it up, 'It is true that a lot of foetus in fetu cases are derived from the same egg but there is no way of knowing at the present if that is the case here. A developing embryo will latch onto anything for a supply of nutrition, even another embryo. Anyway for *Roma*,' he seems to use the name rather pointedly, 'the whole concept of male and female is essentially blurred.'

Milan has the feeling Strangelove is trying to protect him. The concept of Roma being male has indeed rather shocked him. Maybe this is how his parents felt when they saw him for the first time? Milan decides to dismiss the thought outright.

Strangelove quickly turns the conversation into the main area of concern which is to do with Roma learning how to open her eye. It is eventually decided that they will need to physically train her in the first instance.

The operation is scheduled for the Hammersmith. Strangelove apparently had surgeons from Australia and America offering to do the operation, flying over at their own expense.

'We could have sold tickets for the privilege of attending this spectacle,' he tells Milan.

Milan wakes up after the operation in a cloud of morphine feeling slightly bruised and vaguely hallucinating. Roma has already been talking to Strangelove for five minutes. Apparently she likes the morphine and wants more. Tough.

In the night Milan examines his side. The small tube has a protective cap over the end at the minute. Milan is feeling a bit like the bionic man. The whole Roma business seems dreamlike, which is perhaps something to do with the morphine. Milan hears tapping.

< Roma not good. Roma not good >

Milan responds:

< Milan not good either >

12

Another eight days later the training is to start. Milan is still feeling uncomfortable with the tube. It is not the physical presence of it but something more psychological.

Strangelove explains the procedure yet again, 'We want Roma to learn to control her eyelid in darkness. Scott will use an infrared vision system so that he can insert a probe. When he has it in place you tell Roma *Milan open eye* and he will gently open Roma's eye with the probe. Then you will say *Milan close eye* and we close her eye. We do this a few times and then see if we can get her to do it herself.'

Scott dons the infrared goggles, making him look something like a sci-fi warrior. The lights are switched off. Milan feels a gentle tugging at the tube as he removes the protective cap. After a minute he gives him a sign and Milan taps to Roma:

< Milan open Roma's eye >

Scott gives Milan another sign that he has opened the eye. How he can see up the tiny tube Milan has no idea.

< Milan close Roma's eye >

Scott closes her eye again.

Milan is suddenly aware that this is the first time anything has actually touched Roma. You could say that Milan is touching her all the time but that doesn't really count.

After they have done the procedure only three times Milan gets a message:

< Roma open Roma's eye >

Milan tells Scott to just observe.

'She has opened it,' Scott tells everyone.

< Roma close Roma's eye >

She does it.

She is some smart cookie.

There is a spontaneous round of applause from the group of doctors.

Milan signals < Good > to her. Milan feels uncomfortable with this word. It makes him feel as if he is treating her like a well-behaved dog or a small child.

They are moving much faster than anticipated.

Milan tells her:

< Roma open Roma's eye. New, Roma new >

Milan signals the word < Light > and gives a nod to Scott who directs a very gentle beam of pinkish light towards the tube opening. The whole scenario has a semi-religious feel to it.

Strangelove compounds the feeling by announcing *Let*

there be light in a rather dramatic way. Milan wonders, not for the first time, if they are playing at being God with Roma.

Milan signals < Dark > and the light is switched off.

Immediately Milan receives the message:

< Light >

They switch it on again.

Then:

< Dark >

Then:

< Light >

Then:

< Dark >

This continues maybe forty or fifty times. In the pinkish glow Milan can see mounting excitement in the faces gathered around. It almost feels like a séance where they have contacted a spirit.

The doctors had not anticipated getting this far on day one and had failed to prepare for the next step of using different coloured filters.

Suddenly Roma tells Milan she is tired. The cap is replaced and the lights are switched back on. A strange atmosphere pervades the room. A kind of conspiracy has taken place and although the group should be elated they are strangely subdued, as if they are all rather moved.

On his way home on the tube Milan tries to think what it must be like for her.

What would be a comparable experience for him? Eating his first strawberry? The first time he heard music? His first kiss of course. So many firsts seem to happen without due reverence or preparation or appreciation, just in the hustle of everyday life. Milan thinks back to children and how we just thrust things on them. Well maybe not all the time.

Milan makes tea and starts reminiscing about that special occasion when you are going out with someone and you discover they have never been to a certain place before or seen a certain film or never tasted something you really like.

Light, what? You've never seen light before? You've got to try it. It's great. Even better than sound? Well not exactly better, just different. And then you have to say – *I'm really jealous of you, I wish I hadn't seen light before and it was my first time too.* And then when you see it again, it's not quite as good as you remembered and afterward they always say, *Yep, it wasn't bad that light thing. I still prefer sound though* and you have to say, *Well that wasn't the best light I ever saw.*

Next day from the time Milan wakes up all he hears is:

< Light, light. Roma wants light >

Milan answers her:

< Later. Light later >

They get to the clinic at ten.

Scott has a whole array of optical stuff this time. He will not get caught unprepared again. He has dispensed with the infrared goggles. He puts on a low level white light.

Milan tells Roma:

< Eye shut >

Scott removes the cap.

Milan taps:

< Eye open. White light >

Milan taps:

< Dark >

They switch off the light. Scott puts a series of coloured filters over the tube.

< Red light, blue light, green light >

In ten minutes Roma knows her rainbow. She shows a preference for blue. Milan thinks back to Murri striking out the word *blue* from his list and her many attempts to explain the word in metaphors. Well now, Milan thinks a touch triumphantly, this is proper blue, not just something it is like or might remind you of; this is the real thing.

As so many times before Milan is completely staggered by the idea of what must be going on in Roma's head. *Blue* to him is completely wrapped up with blue objects: sky, cold, sea. For Roma *blue* is a pure experience unaffected by anything else.

Scott fits a small lens on the end of the tube.

'I just made a rough guess at the type of lens. We can refine it later if necessary.'

He holds up a card with a black square on it two feet from the end of the tube.

< Square > Milan taps.

< OK, that's a square >

Then a black circle.

No problem.

Scott holds up a triangle, and before Milan can tap in to her he gets back:

< Triangle >

Milan tells the doctors that she already knew it. They are as astounded as he is.

Although he knew Murri had attempted teaching geometry to Roma, Milan had never been convinced that Roma really knew what Murri was talking about. For a second Milan feels like contacting Murri to tell her. Maybe Roma could have guessed *blue* if Milan had given her time.

Roma also figures out *rectangle* with no prompting. They test her on the whole set of shapes. She is one hundred percent correct.

Brave new world Milan thinks.

Scott starts her on letters. Half of Milan's mind is concentrating on tapping them in to her and the other is flying ahead. Whole worlds seem to be literally opening up, pictures of himself, pictures of herself, video films, the Eiffel Tower, paintings, reading. Milan is thinking how much easier it will be to show her things instead of describing them, especially with no other references. *A picture is worth a thousand words* they say. We are going to the pictures, the two of us, Milan thinks, in more ways than one.

They have got to the letter *m* when Milan suddenly realises something is wrong.

Milan is getting a kind of incoherent tapping.

Milan recognises < No > a few times and < Pain > and < Dark > and many confused non-words.

Milan gets Scott to put the cap of the tube back on.

There is a long, long silence from Roma.

They debate the situation.

Strangelove's hypothesis is sensory overload. Perhaps they are going too fast. They decide to call it a day.

The next few days are a nightmare. Roma is rambling and incoherent. By day three she is finally making more sense. She then flatly refuses the light games for a week and a half. Then she agrees to try them again. This time Strangelove has Milan wired up with neural sensors all over his back and stomach. They are OK for less than ten minutes until they enter the crisis again.

Strangelove analyses the readings from the electrodes.

He eventually comes up with the theory that the light is provoking a form of epilepsy in Roma.

Milan is fairly sure that this avenue of development is over. They decide to try gentler experiments when Roma agrees to them again, but Milan knows deep inside this will not happen. Not only in her tapping but through his blood Milan can feel the anguish, the distress.

One for all and all for one.

13

I T is Hyde Park. It is a crisp September morning.

Milan is walking towards Piccadilly to give a lesson.

He gets a message from mission control.

< Can Roma speak to Mozart, please? >

Milan has to sit down for this one. He especially likes the *please*, she hardly ever says *please*.

< Wait a minute > he taps back.

OK, let me think where this is coming from, he says to himself.

Roma is now conscious that there are various beings around. She is aware that beings write music; she writes music, Milan writes music, well he has tried – he even played her some; she was polite. She knows that Mozart writes music. She talks to Milan. Why not talk to Mozart? It is all perfectly logical. In fact Milan wouldn't mind asking Mozart a few questions himself. The immediate question for him however is how to respond? Directly, as always, Milan decides. She is after all a grown woman, at least in one sense of the word.

< Roma can't speak to Mozart because Mozart is dead >

< What dead mean? >

< Mozart begins being two hundred and forty years before now. Mozart stops two hundred years before now >

This is the best Milan can do with the dates; they are not his strong point.

A long silence from Roma. Milan is going to be late, but he thinks he needs to sit this one out.

Eventually Milan hears back from her.

< When does Roma start being? >

< Roma starts forty-two years before now >

Milan remembers Murri spending quite a bit of effort on time, in minutes, hours, right up to years. Milan thinks also of all that careful work on multiplication and sums. It is almost as if Murri had been constructing a person. She used to say that a child without disabilities has so many sources of information that if you leave something out it will be filled in from elsewhere. In her work she is the main conduit for the children. If she forgets something it may leave a gap that might take a very long time to get filled and in certain cases might not.

< When does Roma end? >

< Roma ends twenty years after now or thirty years after now or forty years. Milan does not know >

< Roma will end? >

< Yes. Roma will end >

< Milan will end? >

< Yes >

< Murri will end? >

< Yes >

Silence.

Milan is reminded of the time not so long ago when he sat looking at his notes at the doctor's and saw the space for his date and place of death. Roma never knew about death 'til now, how could she? She would never have known if Milan hadn't told her. He has introduced her mortality to her. He comforts himself by thinking he would rather know about it than not. In addition, in a way, he has reintroduced it to himself. He has forgotten how foreign and alien a concept it is, how unnatural, how insulting, how crushing.

< This ending is called death > Milan confirms.

< Death is like the drift? >

Roma now knows the word *sleep* but continues to use *drift* instead. Milan has never corrected her; it seemed appropriate, poetic even.

< Yes >

Milan is busy congratulating himself on how good he is at communicating such complex metaphysical concepts when he hears more tapping.

< When does Mozart wake up? >

Oh well, Milan thinks, Roma wasn't built in a day.

During the lesson Milan can't concentrate. He sets his

pupil Maxim off on a series of scales and exercises to give himself thinking space. Milan is hit with a wave of panic. What if something happens to him, a stroke or a heart attack, an accident of some kind? Milan supposes he could be kept going on a sort of life support machine, and Roma could carry on. Milan needs to carry a card, like a kidney donor thing, well the opposite of that – Roma would need his kidneys – and the rest. Milan would be donating his whole body to her. Also the card would need to tell them who to contact, Murri? Milan decides to sort it all out after the Vienna trip. With a bump he realises that Maxim has finished and is looking at him expectantly.

'Good, very good, let's have a run through of the Bach slow movement.'

Milan sits down at the piano and gets out the accompaniment for the concerto. Maybe playing will help him concentrate for a least part of the lesson.

They go through the piece with Maxim faultless. He is Milan's star pupil, headed for the Royal Academy no doubt. Milan is about to congratulate him when he hears a tapping.

< Mistake >

< Where? >

< Violin, note ninety-seven, F natural, not F sharp >

Roma has a way of counting the notes in pieces of music these days; you can say Beethoven's *Moonlight Sonata* and she will come back Rain Man-like with fifteen thousand and forty three notes or something. Milan has never actually checked by counting but he somehow believes her – anyway it can be hard to find the place in the music she is talking about. Milan decides to set Maxim off on the hunt.

'You made a mistake. You played an F sharp instead of an F natural. See if you can find it.'

Maxim starts looking through the music and Milan roughly calculates where note ninety-seven might be.

'There are no F naturals in the whole thing,' Maxim responds eventually.

Milan points to the note he has found by counting.

'That's an F sharp,' Maxim shakes his head, 'And look in the accompaniment there is an F sharp; it would clash if I played the natural.'

'What about this little number – there is a footnote here, look, it says in the original manuscript Bach mistakenly wrote an F natural.'

'Yeh, it says *mistakenly*.'

'Let's try it the way Bach wrote it from the bar before.'

They play the section tentatively. It sounds terrible.

'Definitely wrong,' Maxim pronounces.

< Play it properly > Milan hears from inside.

'Let's try it again but this time play it as if you are completely sure that the F natural is right,' Milan asks.

Maxim closes his eyes for a few moments to focus and

then nods. They play the section. It sounds amazing; they carry on to the end – the whole movement is transformed by the one note. Maxim smiles broadly.

Milan takes up his pencil and corrects both their parts firmly, 'JS doesn't make mistakes.'

'What's that called with the natural and sharp at the same time?' Maxim asks, still smiling.

Milan has a feeling he is being fed a line but answers, 'It's called a false relation.'

Maxim nods, 'I've got an uncle who is always telling lies.'

Milan sighs.

'It's also known as a cross relation and…please don't bother telling me about your bad-tempered auntie.'

'Oh, you know her then.'

The rehearsals have stepped up in the week leading to the Austrian tour. Daphne has a new book, *The Young Paganini*. She reads Milan an extract in her soft northern accent, 'Paganini was fond of and may even have invented the technique of Fleischton. This is the practice where the violinist uses the fleshy part of the finger to stop the note rather than the callused tip of the finger thereby producing a particularly sweet sound. The technique must be used sparingly as on the one hand it is extremely painful, especially on the very high notes, and secondly if overused then that part of the finger also becomes callused and the effect is lost. "Just as in life and love" the young Paganini would comment.'

'*Fleischton*?' Milan has never heard of that before.

'Nor me,' Daphne answers.

Milan gets his violin out, 'Let me try it.'

Milan goes up to the top of his E string with a flat finger. It certainly is painful.

'Does this sound sweeter to you? Or this?'

Milan plays the normal way.

'Again.'

'Close your eyes,' Milan tells her.

After five minutes they are undecided. His fingers are definitely decided. Milan is glad it doesn't produce any noticeable effect.

'He probably just made it up for the ladies, ' Daphne agrees.

For the ladies – she says *ladies* like *liedees*.

Milan nods in agreement and then remembers the lesson with Maxim.

'Say, Daphne, you know this Bach slow movement?' he plays the opening bars.

'Duh, of course, I am a professional violinist remember.'

'Listen to this bit,' Milan plays the section with the false relation.

'You need to work on your bowing a bit, and you made a mistake; it's F sharp not natural.'

'Not in the original manuscript.'

'Nobody plays it the way you just did. I must have heard it in twenty versions. Why do you think it's that way?'

'Roma told me.'

'But she could never have heard it like that.'

Milan shrugs.

'You need to hear it like this with the accompaniment. The whole movement is, what's the word, transfigured.'

'How did she tell you?'

'In a lesson, she's started correcting my pupils for me.'

'Well I'm glad she's earning her keep at last.'

The orchestra stiffens uncomfortably as their latest guest conductor noisily enters the hall.

'Maybe she could give Vlad the Impaler here a couple of tips.'

After the rehearsal walking down Regent Street Milan bumps into Karen holding hands with a Japanese guy.

'This is Hitoshi. Hitoshi this is Milan,' she introduces them in a somewhat distant fashion.

Milan bows in a weird way.

'Konichiwa,' he says.

'He Korean,' Karen informs Milan, a little unkindly he thinks.

Hitoshi is smiling anyway.

'He doesn't speak any English.'

Hitoshi speaks to Karen.

'He want to talk to Roma. She quite famous in Korea. All his family would be very impressed.'

Milan is glad of Hitoshi's presence. The last time Milan saw Karen she was doing up her blouse complaining of

Roma's prudishness. And the whole business of Murri; it doesn't bear thinking about.

'Sure thing. First of all I will introduce him to Roma.'

Milan taps out saying out loud at the same time, 'This is Hitoshi from Korea, a long way away. He is a friend of Karen who is also here.'

Meanwhile Karen is busy translating into Korean.

Milan gets a response from his sister and tells them, 'Greetings Hitoshi from far away. I am Roma. What music do you like?'

They go round the houses translationally and Milan is struck by the doubleness of the translation.

Hitoshi answers Messiaen eventually.

He asks if he can hear Roma speak and as there is a problem with the speaker on the belt Milan lets him put his hand on his back. They are causing a bit of a pedestrian blockage on the pavement and Milan is aware of the stares at what must after all be a strange sight – a Korean groping an Englishman in broad daylight on the Queen's highway.

They eventually end up in a welter of greetings and farewells. Hitoshi is very pleased and is smiling.

'Have a good life,' is Karen's final remark to Milan and indeed it does seem rather final. What else should he expect, after all?

That evening Roma tells Milan:

< There are one hundred and forty-seven >

< One hundred and forty-seven what? >

< Roma, Milan, Hitoshi, Karen, Mozart, Andreas, Murri, Beethoven... > She goes on with the list, they are mostly composers.

Milan stops her:

< Roma, there are more than that >

< How many? >

Milan takes a deep breath. This is going to tax his numerical skills:

< Six times a hundred times a hundred times... > Milan spells out the six billion.

A pause, then:

< Six plus a hundred plus a hundred ...? >

< No. Not plus, times >

A very long pause. Then:

< What are their names? >

At times like this Milan wishes Murri was around.

14

Next day they are off to Vienna. Milan is sitting next to Daphne on the plane.

'Why give up the habits of a lifetime?' she had remarked as she eased into the seat next to him. When they are up in the air they rise quickly above the clouds. The sun is so bright Milan can hardly look out of the window. He is reminded of that old saying that the sun is always shining, only it's just that when it's cloudy you can't see it. Everything Milan thinks about seems to relate to Roma. He is her clouds.

Daphne brings him down to earth with a bump, 'You off on one? Don't want these do you?' She takes a handful of his peanuts. She makes the most of her plane journeys. She has already persuaded the steward to give her two vodka and tonics.

'She got a passport?' nodding at his midriff.

'That's a thought.'

'You are going to smuggle an illegal alien into Austria.'

'It's a foolproof way to do it.'

Daphne pushes her seat back under the influence of her vodkas. The people behind make complaining noises which she ignores.

Outside the cloud has cleared and Milan can see mountains and German – or is it Swiss? – towns. Milan wonders about mentioning the fact that they are three thousand feet above the ground and travelling at four hundred miles an hour to his sister but it is one of those many things that are almost meaningless. It is a bit like the fact that on earth we are all flying through space at God knows how many zillion miles an hour but completely unaware of the fact. Milan is now Roma's earth instead of her clouds. On a more practical level Milan uses the example of Daphne to get him and Roma two gin and tonics as well, one each.

They circle Vienna airport for twenty minutes. Daphne is engrossed in another book. Milan recalls Lisa's opinion that he should read stories to Roma. He asks Daphne's advice, 'What would be a good book to read to my sister?'

She rummages in the bag under her seat and pulls out a tatty old paperback.

'You could try this. I just finished it. It made me cry, if that's any recommendation.'

Milan looks at the cover. It is *The Heart is a Lonely Hunter* by Carson McCullers. He has never read it but the title sounds familiar.

As they are coming down the steps of the plane George embarrassingly breaks into *Vienna* by Ultravox. He is quickly stifled by the musical members of the orchestra. A special bus takes them to a craggy old hotel right in the middle of the city.

After unpacking Milan decides to have a wander on his own. He ends up at the big cathedral in the middle of the town and has a look inside. Milan is surprised to see Daphne kneeling, obviously praying. Milan is just about to beat a hasty retreat when he catches her eye. Daphne jumps up brushing herself down and comes over to him, smiling in an embarrassed kind of way.

'I didn't know you were religious?' Milan asks her.

She wrinkles her nose, 'Just keeping my options open, you know.'

'Don't say that in here, he's bound to be listening. Coffee?'

Outside it is getting dark.

'Are you religious yourself then?' Daphne asks in turn.

'Never given it much thought.'

'What about Roma?'

'Roma worships the holy trinity of fags, booze and chocolate.'

'You must seem a bit like a god to her. She can't see you, she asks for things and sometimes you let her have them. You know everything and you can make things happen, if you want to.'

'For a god I don't get that much respect.'

Milan is reminded of Strangelove's *let there be light* announcement. Well in that case at least, he thinks, if we were gods, we weren't that successful.

That evening the orchestra heads into town for a session of serious drinking. Milan has instead decided to set aside a little quality time with Roma in his hotel room. They have a brand new duty-free bottle of whisky and Daphne's paperback.

< I am going to read you a book > Milan taps out. The book looks rather long. Milan thinks maybe he should have started with something easier? He worries about repetitive strain injury with all that tapping.

< What is book? >

Book? She doesn't know the word *book*? Murri said she would have surprising gaps in her knowledge but this seems more like a Grand Canyon than a gap. How do you describe a book? With a small child it is so easy; you just stick one in their tiny hands. They turn the pages, look at the pictures, see the words and you read it with them. Book, simple, no problemo.

< Forget about word book. I am going to tell you a story, things about some people. It's not true >

Milan doesn't want her to actually think these people are really running around out here, does he?

< It's a lie? >

< No, not exactly a lie. It's like when you make up music. Only this time with words. A composition of words, OK? >

< OK >

< The title is *The Heart is a Lonely Hunter* >

< What is heart? >

< Heart is that thing you hear going... >

Milan taps an imitation heart rhythm.

< It pushes blood round >

< Blood? >

Every word seems to rely on another word. It's like building on sand trying to explain them.

< We'll come back to blood later. Anyway, heart stands for something else >

< A metaphor? >

What? She doesn't know *book* but she knows *metaphor?* Milan used to wonder what Murri and Roma were gabbling about at three o'clock in the morning.

< Yes, a metaphor. Heart stands for love >

< I love Murri >

Oh, do you then? Time to turn the tables.

Milan taps out:

< What is love? >

Short pause.

< Love is where you are very sad when you can't talk to someone any more >

Ouch! Milan had asked. Let's move on, he thinks.

< The heart is a lonely hunter > he repeats.

< Hunter? >

< Someone who looks for something very hard >

< Lonely? >

< How you feel when someone you love is not there >

< I like this story >

Well that's a good start; they haven't even got to page one yet. Milan opens up at the first chapter and taps in:

< In the town there were two mutes, and they were always together >

< Mutes? >

< People who can't talk out loud >

< Like me? >

< Yes, just like you >

< I like this story >

15

THE first concert goes surprisingly well despite the fact that the orchestra has a massive collective hangover and that they are playing Mahler in Vienna. It's like taking coals to Newcastle, but on the other hand as George says it's the only music the Viennese know. If they played Elgar or Purcell it would be to themselves. At least with the Mahler the Viennese come to see how badly they do it, a bit like Daphne's dog walking on two legs.

The day after the concert the violins are taken en masse to the Klimt museum. Milan doesn't know where the rest of the orchestra have gone, probably to a bar.

Milan detaches himself from the crowd and wanders around on his own describing the paintings as best he can to Roma. Milan has developed a way of folding his arms over his stomach so that you can hardly see his hand tapping to her. The trouble is when someone does notice it, it looks as if Milan is bored and fidgety. He sees a few of the rich Viennese giving him strange looks.

Roma is becoming quite an art connoisseur these days, from his descriptions she can recognise quite a few artists, Van Gogh, Picasso, Klimt now. Many of the pictures here are so amazing Milan has that old twinge of wishing she could really see. Milan touches the place where the viewing tube had been; the doctors had been able to remove the stent fairly easily. Anyway, maybe she is seeing the pictures in her imagination even more vividly than they actually are, Milan consoles himself, like when people compare television to radio.

At the end of their last Austrian rehearsal, two days before they are due to go back to London, the orchestra breaks into *Happy Birthday*. It is surprisingly atonal and dissonant for professional musicians. When they get to the names they have to bolt to get the *RomaandMilan* in. Milan finds himself rather touched. He looks at Daphne who is the obvious culprit, but she merely shrugs.

Milan realises that he hasn't told Roma that it is her birthday and that the subject hasn't even cropped up before. Sometimes when Murri has explained things to Roma without him noticing, Milan gets a tart reply back of < I know that!! > Milan doesn't think so in this case.

He takes the plunge:

< Roma, today is our birthday >

< Birthday, what is that? >

< It is a celebration of the day we were born >

< What is being born? >

Another fine mess he's gotten himself into.

< Being born is when you are made. Another person, your mother, makes you inside themselves and when you come out it is called being born >

< But I am inside you still? >

This is obviously why Murri steered clear of this area.

< We should have come out together. We did in fact come out of our mother together. Only you got stuck inside me >

< Can I come out now? >

< If you came out you would die. Sorry >

< It's OK, I'm happy here >

< Happy birthday Roma >

< Happy birthday Milan >

Maybe one day all the different things will start joining up for her and make up a bigger picture instead of all these dislocated pieces of information. When Milan first moved to London he got the tube everywhere. He would pop up in Tottenham Court Road, then in Covent Garden and so on and never realised where they were in relation to each other. Only when Milan started walking around did he realise how all the places he knew quite well connected together.

Daphne has a birthday treat for Milan and Roma. That afternoon she takes them to the Riesenrad on the Prater where they made *The Third Man*. When they are up on top of the big ferris wheel they try to open the door to look out like in the film but the door is firmly locked. Milan does the cuckoo clock speech anyway and then Daphne informs him that Orson does that speech after he gets out again at the bottom. When he is in the cabin he is talking about people as if they were ants and *who would care if one stopped moving?*

Next morning after their last rehearsal George volunteers to take Milan shopping. George is one quarter Swiss and speaks German like a native.

'Have you taught Roma any foreign languages?'

Milan shakes his head, 'I'm trying to keep it simple, for me as much as her. She knows *konichiwa* but the extent of her German is *schnapps* and *Budweiser*.'

'Maybe she has her own language that she used before you started communicating?'

'I can't imagine what that would be like.'

'King James of Scotland, didn't he put a load of children on an island with a nanny who couldn't speak, to see what language they would end up with?'

'What did they?'

'Can't honestly remember. I don't think it turned out well. Also there were all those children brought up by wolves and such.'

George buys a box of chocolates.

'Mozart Kugel,' he tells Milan, 'which translates as *Mozart's balls*.'

'Nice,' Milan replies.

'*Balls* doesn't mean *balls* in German. *Balls*, as they say, are called *eggs* here.'

Milan has started tapping to Roma.

'You explaining about the *balls* thing?'

'No, I was just telling her that chocolate is coming her way. I don't think she knows about balls, or maybe Murri told her while I was asleep. She does know that there are men and women.'

'What about swearing? Does she swear?'

'I think she learnt a few from Murri.'

'Such as?'

'*Shit, bum, arse*.'

'Does she know what those words really mean?'

'I expect she knows something of *shit* though it's not the concept we understand, more of a relief thing, coupled with exotic sound effects I imagine. *Bum* and *arse* I don't think so.'

'Just pure swearing then?'

'I guess so.'

They start to cross the street. Milan hears shouting in German and a metallic screeching.

16

MILAN wakes up early in the morning. It is around seven o'clock. A car horn blares five times and then stops and then starts again. Something is different – in fact a lot is different. Milan looks at the ceiling. It seems closer than normal in the autumn half-light. A cold wave of unease passes through him.

Milan taps a short message:

< Is Roma there? Hello Milan here >

Nothing comes back. Perhaps she is sleeping. Perhaps she is cross. She has refused to speak to him before. Milan closes his eyes but does not sleep. A sharp pain hits him and he cries out involuntarily.

A nurse bends over him, she says something in German and hurries away. She returns quickly with someone in a white coat.

'Mr Kotzia, you are back with us.' He has a German accent.

'Where am I?' Even as he says it Milan realises how corny it sounds.

'You are in our hospital – you and your friend walked out in front of a tram.'

'George, my friend, is he all right?'

The doctor takes his wrist to feel his pulse and maybe to distract Milan or himself.

'No, I'm afraid he is not all right. Not at all right.'

'He's dead?'

'Yes, that is sadly the case. He took the main force of the collision. You however were lucky, doubly so in fact. Firstly, your injuries were far less severe and secondly while you were under surgery we discovered a large and unusual tumour that could have been very dangerous to you, but I am glad to say we managed to remove it safely.'

Milan lies very still. He lies very still.

Eventually his mouth moves on its own.

'My sister is dead, you mean. You killed her.'

The doctor looks at the nurse who shrugs.

'There was no one else involved, only you and your friend. You had a visitor but I am sure she was not your sister and she is very much alive.'

Milan is crying.

The nurse gives him an injection and he falls asleep.

When he wakes again Daphne is sitting at his bedside. She is holding his hand.

He looks at her, 'You know?'

'I explained everything about Roma to them. The surgeon is devastated.'

'I want to take her body back to England.'

'I guessed you would. I told them. They're making all the arrangements.'

George's wife suddenly appears at the bottom of Milan's bed like a ghost. She has one of their young boys with her.

She looks at him with a quizzical expression, 'I expect he was too busy talking to look where he was going?'

Milan nods slowly.

'Stupid fool.' She turns away and walks with the boy towards the door.

'Hope you get better soon,' she says without looking round.

'She all right?' Milan asks Daphne.

'Her brother is over with her.'

'That's nice, having a brother to look after you, isn't it?'

'I'm so sorry about Roma.'

Milan notices that Daphne is crying as she speaks.

17

MILAN goes to see Dr Strangelove.

He sits down. Neither says anything for a long time. A pencil rolls off the desk.

Neither moves.

Eventually Strangelove breaks the silence.

'We need to find out the implications for you.'

'For me?'

'Yes, for you. No man is an island, as they say, especially in your case.'

Milan sits there numb. Strangelove obviously thinks the way out of this tragedy is through practical measures. Maybe he is right. Milan seems to remember saying the island thing to Professor Conway a long time ago.

'We can start with blood tests and then more scans.'

Milan goes along with the game.

Milan gives some blood samples and gets back into the white tube.

By early evening Dr Strangelove pronounces himself happy with Milan's health.

'I don't think we should do anything at the minute. They did a good re-arranging job in there, those Austrian boys. Normally a large cavity would have been left.'

Milan hardly listens. A large cavity has been left but he doesn't say that. Instead he nods.

Strangelove tidies his papers before saying,

'I'll need to see you tomorrow.'

Milan wanders out into the dusk. He is tapping unconsciously on his hipbone.

< Night, rain > Did she ever truly understand rain?

< Go home, hungry? >

Strangely, Milan has reverted to their earlier clipped baby conversations, the ones that were theirs alone.

Milan stops himself and then wonders why he stopped.

He would like to tap out *goodbye* but it's not a word they ever used, not a word he thought they would ever need. Milan remembers Murri using it that last time they saw each other and he has a tiny pang of guilt. Maybe he was too hard on her about the research business; it was certainly too hard on the innocent Roma. He wonders, could anyone have been more innocent than Roma? Was she a good person? Was she selfish? How could she have been anything but selfish? And what does all that good and bad stuff mean if you have no power?

Back at the flat Milan puts on some music. It seems void.

He gets his violin out. Its tones annoy him. Maybe he is just so depressed that he can't take music in. But somewhere he has the feeling that he will never really enjoy music again, that it wasn't actually him who liked it, who pumped the soothing chemicals into his blood stream on hearing a favourite piece. He was a surrogate musician.

Milan goes back to Strangelove's office next morning.

'I want a death certificate.'

Strangelove is very patient. He nearly says that Roma didn't officially exist. He checks himself.

'We don't have anything to...'

'You have a dead body.'

'Didn't the Austrians give you something?'

'They didn't want to admit to culpability. If Roma had died then they had killed her.'

'I see.'

Strangelove takes up a pad. He fills it in carefully. He asks Milan questions. He stamps it. He hands it over. It is not a death certificate but a request to the registry office to issue a birth certificate.

'Arriving is more important than leaving,' he says kindly.

Milan looks at the piece of paper.

'Are you allowed to do this? Won't you get in trouble?'

'What will they do? Sack me? Anyway all I'm doing is correcting another doctor's mistake. Two people were born but the doctor only noticed one.'

Milan folds the letter carefully and thanks this good doctor.

Milan sits for several hours in the park on his way home, thoughts buzzing round and round in his head. He can't make sense of it, things going along from day to day and then suddenly stopping, all change. It's not like in a film or a book or something where you can see what's coming, where things happen for a reason, for a structure.

Milan takes out the battered McCullers paperback. After a fairly slow start they had been romping through it. Whenever Milan had had a minute in a rehearsal in Vienna, or in the hotel bath, he would get a request for more story, more explanations. In a way this parallel world of the *Lonely Hunter* book had been as real to Roma as the outside world that Milan was describing to her. Except Ms McCullers has a better way with words than him, so it could be that the writer's world was even more vivid to Roma than his.

Roma. She was a star blasting out energy and light into his world and she is now a tiny black hole in his life sucking away his feelings.

Milan wonders if in another parallel universe maybe it is him who is inside a Roma who has just discovered him tapping.

Over the next few days Murri calls several times and leaves messages on the answer machine. Milan wonders how she has heard. She sounds genuinely upset, more than upset, devastated. Well that puts the lid on that piece of research, Milan thinks unkindly. He doesn't return her calls.

There are quite a few people who come to the door but Milan doesn't answer. He notices that it will be three days 'til the one-year anniversary of the first tapping. Milan thinks how strange that they were forty-two years with each other and yet only one short year together.

On the anniversary three days later Milan hires a car and goes down to the countryside near Epping. He buries the little box containing Roma and plants a tiny sycamore tree on top. As Milan pats the earth a flood of tears escapes from him for the first time since he came back to England, surprising him with its suddenness. He realises he was trying to think of describing the word *tree*, never mind *sycamore* to Roma.

Milan seems to have been in an emotional vacuum over the past years, skating on the surface of life as if he has just been watching a film of himself all this time, a film that he didn't really care much about. He is reminded of that Laurel and Hardy film where they go to Oxford and the skinny one gets hit on the head with a window and becomes brainy. Then at the end he gets hit again and goes back to normal. Maybe Roma's death is Milan's second hit.

He tidies up the grass around the tree. He has made a memorial that would have meant nothing to the person honoured. Under the tree Milan lays out a single flower and the paperback and the tiny cassette player that he bought for her all that time ago. Then on a second thought he takes back the book and puts it in his pocket – maybe he needs it more than she does. He turns the cassette player on. It is the middle movement of the Mozart clarinet concerto.

Milan walks back to the car leaving the music playing softly into the afternoon.